NERO CARACAS—THE ASSASSIN. POLO HERO, NATIONAL ICON, THE WORLD'S MOST ELIGIBLE BACHELOR AND MOST BEDDABLE MAN. THE HEARTBREAKER OF ARGENTINA.

When he dipped his head, one professional acknowledging another, she saw the steel of challenge in his eyes. Nero Caracas was hardly the most sensible enemy for a woman in Bella's precarious financial position to make.

But she wouldn't fail, Bella told herself firmly, straightening up to confront this god of the game. 'Is that everything?'

Nero's lips pressed down. 'No,' he said with a shake of his head. 'I think Misty would benefit from being ridden by a man who really appreciates her.'

'I can assure you that the captain of the English team appreciates Misty—'

'But does he ride her in a way that brings Misty pleasure?'

Did Nero Caracas have to make everything sound like an invitation to bed?

Susan Stephens was a professional singer before meeting her husband on the tiny Mediterranean island of Malta. In true Modern™ Romance style they met on Monday, became engaged on Friday, and were married three months after that. Almost thirty years and three children later, they are still in love. (Susan does not advise her children to return home one day with a similar story, as she may not take the news with the same fortitude as her own mother!)

Susan had written several non-fiction books when fate took a hand. At a charity costume ball there was an after-dinner auction. One of the lots, 'Spend a Day with an Author', had been donated by Mills & Boon® author Penny Jordan. Susan's husband bought this lot, and Penny was to become not just a great friend but a wonderful mentor, who encouraged Susan to write romance.

Susan loves her family, her pets, her friends and her writing. She enjoys entertaining, travel, and going to the theatre. She reads, cooks, and plays the piano to relax, and can occasionally be found throwing herself off mountains on a pair of skis or galloping through the countryside. Visit Susan's website: www.susanstephens.net.

Praise for
Susan Stephens:

ITALIAN BOSS, PROUD MISS PRIM
'Stephens' terrific story shows how love can be transforming. The marvellous hero looks beyond the surface and frees the heroine to open up about her biggest fears.'

—RT Book Reviews

'You can always rely on Susan Stephens to deliver a steamy, sexy, fast-paced emotional page-turner, and RULING SHEIKH, UNRULY MISTRESS certainly does not disappoint.'

—Cataromance

THE UNTAMED ARGENTINIAN

BY
SUSAN STEPHENS

First published in Great Britain 2011
by Mills & Boon, an imprint of Harlequin (UK) Limited,
Eton House, 18-24 Paradise Road, Richmond, Surrey TW9 1SR

© Susan Stephens 2011

ISBN: 978 0 263 22059 9

Harlequin (UK) policy is to use papers that are natural, renewable
and recyclable products and made from wood grown in sustainable
forests. The logging and manufacturing process conform to the
legal environmental regulations of the country of origin.

Printed and bound in Great Britain
by CPI Antony Rowe, Chippenham, Wiltshire

THE UNTAMED
ARGENTINIAN

CHAPTER ONE

'Do you mind if I join you?'

A shiver of recognition ran down Bella's back as the man with the husky Latin American voice lifted the latch on the stable door and walked in. There was only one man who could breeze through security in Her Majesty's backyard: the Guards' Polo Club in Windsor. Nero Caracas, known as the Assassin in polo circles, played off ten, the highest ranking a polo player could achieve, and enjoyed privileges around the world others could only dream of. Impossibly good-looking, Bella had seen Nero commanding the field of play, and had lusted after him like every other hot-blooded woman, but nothing could have prepared her to be this close to so much man.

'So this is Misty,' he said, running an experienced palm down the pony's shoulder. 'She looks smaller close up—'

'Appearances can be deceptive.' Racing to the defence of her favourite pony, Bella forced her hands to go on oiling the mare's dainty hooves. She'd lived close to animals for so long she was as acutely tuned in to danger as they were and, though the mare seemed calm, Bella was on red alert.

'The match starts soon—'

And? Bella thought, still polishing. As trainer and one of the coaches of the British team, she knew only too well when the match started. Surely it was Nero, as captain of the opposing team, who should be elsewhere?

Nero's reputation preceded him. He had obviously thought he could drop in and his smallest wish would be granted with one eye on the timetable for a match in which he would captain the Argentinian team. No such luck. The Assassin could yield to the Ice Maiden on this occasion. And he did, but with a warning glint in his eye. 'I need to speak to you about Misty,' he said, running another appreciative glance over her pony.

'This isn't the time,' Bella said coolly, realising only when their stares clashed that she was running the same type of assessing look over Nero—experience had nothing to do with it. Her points of reference were in her head. And all the better for staying there, she thought, having taken in Nero's dark tan, close-fitting white breeches, plain dark polo shirt, wayward curls catching on his ferocious black stubble, not to mention the leather boots hugging his hard-muscled calves. It was safer, certainly.

'As you wish,' he said.

When he dipped his head, one professional acknowledging another, she saw the steel of challenge in his eyes. Nero Caracas was hardly the most sensible enemy for a woman in Bella's precarious financial position to make. The recession had taken a deep bite out of her resources and the polo world was too small, too incestuous to take chances. You failed in the eyes of one, you failed in the eyes of everyone. But she wouldn't fail, Bella told herself firmly, straightening up to confront this god of the game. 'Is that everything?'

Nero's lips pressed down. 'No,' he said with a shake

of his head. 'I think Misty would benefit from being ridden by a man who really appreciates her—'

'I can assure you that the captain of the English team appreciates Misty—'

'But does he ride her in a way that brings Misty pleasure?'

Did Nero Caracas have to make everything sound like an invitation to bed?

She glanced at her watch.

'Do I make you nervous, Bella?'

She laughed. 'Certainly not—I'm merely concerned that you're leaving yourself dangerously short of time.'

'My timing is split second,' Nero assured her.

Was that humour in his eyes? As the rugged Argentinian caressed Misty's neck, Bella lost herself for a moment. All muscles and tough, virile appeal, Nero Caracas was quite a man. Another woman, another time—who knew what might come of this meeting? Bella thought wryly, dragging herself round.

'En garde,' Nero murmured when she came to stand between him and the dapple grey polo pony. 'I would like you on my side, Isabella, not working against me for the competition.'

Bella gave him an ironic look. 'I'm very happy where I am, thank you.'

'Maybe I can change your mind—'

'I wish you joy of that—'

'If that's a gauntlet, I should warn you, Bella, I always pick them up.'

Too much man—too close—too desperately disturbing...

Irritated by the fact that her highly strung mare had remained calm when Nero had entered the stable, Bella demanded sharply, 'Anything else?'

Sensation overload, she registered dizzily as Nero's long dark stare made her heart go crazy. Nero Caracas was ridiculously attractive and had more charisma than was good for any man. No woman wanted to be reduced to a primal mating state by an unreconstructed male. A woman wanted control—something Bella possessed in vast amounts...usually.

Nero raised his hands in mock surrender. 'Don't worry, I'm going. But I'll be back to see you, Misty,' he crooned to the unusually compliant mare.

Bella's eyes flashed fire. 'When I'm not here, Misty is protected by the most stringent security measures.'

'Which I'll be sure to bear in mind—' Nero's Latin shrug could easily be translated as *So what?*

No one would keep him out. Nero Caracas could do anything he wanted, buy anything he wanted. Chatter around the yard suggested the famous Argentinian wanted to buy Misty, the polo pony Bella had foolishly allowed herself to love.

'You've done well with Misty, Bella,' Nero observed as he paused by the stable door. 'She's in prime condition—'

'Because she's happy with me—'

Nero's head dipped in acknowledgement of this, but the sardonic smile on his lips suggested he had more to offer any horse than she did.

She was at risk of losing Misty. The thought struck Bella like a bombshell. There was always pressure—honour in the game that demanded the best players were given the best polo ponies to ride. Misty was the best, and only a fool would stand in the way of a rider like Nero Caracas and expect to keep the career she loved intact.

'Until the next time, Bella—'

I wouldn't count on it, Bella thought, tightening her lips. There would be no *next time.* Misty was all she had left of her late father's yard—her late father's honour. While Misty was on the field people still talked of Jack Wheeler as the best of trainers, and forgot for that moment that Bella's father had been a gambler who had lost everything he had ever worked for. 'Misty only runs for those she trusts.'

'Like any woman.' Nero's smile deepened, carving an attractive crease in the side of his face. Coming back to the pony, he ran an experienced hand down Misty's near foreleg. 'Good legs,' he commented as he straightened up.

And she felt hers tingling too. The look Nero gave her left Bella in no doubt that everything in the stable had been assessed. She was way out of her depth here. If only Nero would go and everything could return to normal. 'Enjoy the match,' she said numbly, conscious of the power he wielded in the game.

'You too, Bella—' There was both humour and challenge in his voice.

'Misty will outrun your Criolla ponies from the Pampas—'

'We'll see.' Nero shot her an amused glance. 'My Criollo are descendants of the Spanish war horses. Their power is second to none. Their loyalty? Unquestioned. Stamina?' His lips pressed down in the most attractive way. 'Unrivalled, Bella. And it goes without saying that combat is in their genes.'

And Nero's, Bella thought. She'd watched him play, and had marvelled at his speed and agility, his hand-to-eye coordination, uncanny intuition, and the eager way Nero's ponies responded to him. She had never thought she would feel those subtle powers working on her. 'May the best man win,' she said, tilting her chin at a defiant angle as she rested a protective hand on Misty's neck.

'I have no doubt that he will,' the undisputed king of the game informed her.

She had always felt safe in the stables, with the scent of clean hay in her nostrils and the warmth of an animal she could trust close by, but that safety had just been challenged by a man whose voice was like a smoky cellar, deep and evocative, though ultimately cold. Whatever game it was, she must never forget that Nero Caracas always played to win. 'Win or lose today, Misty is not for sale—'

'I've completed my examination, and I like what I see,' Nero remarked as if she hadn't spoken. 'Of course, Misty would need to pass the vet's exam,' he went on thoughtfully, 'but if she fulfils her promise today, as I'm sure she will, I'd like to make you an offer, Bella. Name your price.'

'There is no price, Señor Caracas.' She wasn't going to roll over just because Nero Caracas said she must. 'I don't need your money.'

Nero angled his head. He didn't need to say anything to echo the thoughts of everyone else in the polo world, all of whom knew that couldn't be true. 'You might not need my money, *chica*,' he said with a faint mocking edge to his voice, 'but you must need something. Everybody does…'

'Is that a threat?' Was she to lose everything she had worked for? A flash of panic speared through her as the dark master of the game stared her down. Why should Nero answer when he was the centre of the polo universe, around which everything else revolved? He had more money, more skill on the field and a better eye for the horse than any man alive. Why was she challenging him when Nero Caracas could dash her career against the wall with a flick of his wrist?

'Relax,' he murmured. 'You work too hard and worry too much, Bella. Polo?' The massive shoulders eased in a shrug. 'It's only a game.'

Only a game?

'I look forward to seeing Misty play.' The dark eyes stared deeper into her soul than they had any right to and then he was gone.

Bella let out a shuddering breath and slumped back against the cold stone wall. How could she fight him? But fight him she would if Nero pushed her, Bella determined as one of her grooms came in and, after a few covert sideways glances, asked if Bella was all right.

'I'm fine... Fine,' Bella confirmed, wishing she was back at home with her dogs and horses, where life was uncomplicated, and where the children she encouraged to visit her stable yard learned how to care for animals in a blissfully down-to-earth setting. Mess with Nero and she would lose all that.

'Shall I take Misty to the pony lines?'

The girl glanced towards the stable door as she spoke, and Bella guessed she must have passed the master of the game on his way out. Nero threw off an aura of power and danger, which had made the young girl anxious. 'Yes, take her,' she confirmed, 'but don't let her out of your sight for a moment.'

'I won't,' the girl promised. 'Come on, Misty,' she coaxed, taking hold of the reins.

'Actually, I've changed my mind—I'll come with you.' She had intended to check the other ponies first, but she could do that at the pony lines. Nero Caracas turning up unannounced had really shaken her. He had reminded her that her life was a house of cards that could collapse at any time and that Nero Caracas never paid anyone a visit without a purpose in mind.

She would just have to fight his fire with her ice, Bella concluded, shutting the stable door behind them. She had done it before and come through in one piece. There was still talk about how her father's gambling had destroyed his career, which was one reason she still had the Ice Maiden tag. Life had taught her to keep rigid control over her feelings at all times. And Misty was more than just a pony; the small mare was a symbol of Bella's determination to rebuild the family name. She had promised her father before he died that she would always keep Misty safe. So could she fight off this bid from Nero Caracas?

She had to. Nero might be every woman's dream with his blacksmith's shoulders, wicked eyes and piratical stubble, but she had a job to do.

'Good luck, Bella,' the stable hands chorused as she crossed the yard.

Lifting her hand in recognition of their support, she hurried on, afraid to let Misty out of her sight now.

'The Argentine team is looking good,' one of the grooms observed, keeping pace with her for a few steps. 'Especially Nero Caracas—he's been living up to his nickname in the last few matches. The Assassin has cut a swathe through the competition—'

'Great. Thank you.' She didn't need reminding that Nero inhabited a brutal world. He might feel at home here, and play the role of gentleman in the prince's backyard, but Nero lived in Argentina, where he bred and trained his ponies on an *estancia* the size of a country on the vast untamed reaches of the pampas.

The pampas.

This conjured up such fabulous images—terrifyingly wild and impossibly dangerous.

And the sooner he went back there, the sooner she could relax, Bella told herself firmly. They had reached the pony lines where the horses were tethered to wait their turn to enter the match. 'I'll never let you go,' she whispered, throwing her arms around Misty's firm grey neck. 'And I'd certainly never sell you on to some black-hearted savage like Nero Caracas. Why, I'd sooner—'

The images that conjured up had to stop there. Burying her face against Misty's warm hide, Bella tried and failed to blot out the image of her moaning with pleasure in Nero's arms. Daydreams were one thing, but she'd be sure to lock the stable door in future.

He never listened to gossip. He preferred to make up his own mind about people, places, animals, things—

And Isabella Wheeler.

The Ice Maiden's eyes had been wary and hostile to begin with, but not by the time he had left her. Why was Bella's luscious, long red hair cruelly contained beneath a net? It was preternaturally neat, but he had detected a wild streak beneath that icy veneer. He had seen enough ponies standing meekly in the corral, only to kick the daylights out of a groom if they weren't approached with respect. Control ruled Bella. She had earned the highest respect in equine circles, but still managed to remain an enigma, without a shred of gossip concerning her private life. How could she not present him with a challenge he found impossible to resist?

Mounting up, he gathered his reins and called his team around him for the pep talk. He was unusually wired and the men knew it. They stared at him warily whilst keeping a tight rein on their own restless mounts.

'No mercy,' he warned, 'but don't risk the horses. And take care of the grey the English captain will be riding. Depending on how the grey does today, I might want to buy her—'

Bella wouldn't sell her horse to him?

His determination to change that mounted as he remembered Bella would barely speak to him. The thought of unbuttoning that tightly laced exterior and seeing her eyes beg for pleasure instead of challenging him was all the encouragement he needed. He wanted her to relax for him. He wanted to discover who Bella Wheeler really was—

The light of challenge was so fierce in his eyes that his team, mistaking it for the fire of battle, wheeled away.

Bella would be different. Not easy, Nero thought as he took his helmet off to acknowledge the roar of the crowd when he galloped onto the field. Bella would not yield to him as easily as her pretty mare had. There was something else behind that composed stare. Fear. He wondered at it. She feared the loss of her pony—that he could understand, but there was something more. And there was another question: why did such a successful and attractive woman live the life of a celibate in what was a notoriously libidinous society?

Because Bella was different. She was an independent woman, and courageous. She had coped well with her father's disgrace, supporting Jack Wheeler to the bitter end and salvaging what she could of the business. But where a private life was concerned she seemed to have none, and planned to keep it that way, or why else would she dress so severely?

Bella was all business and no fun, Nero concluded, as if to show the slightest warmth or humour might put her at risk. Yet beneath that Ice Maiden façade he'd heard she was much loved by the children she invited to her stables. She could be useful to him. With that thought in mind, he replaced his helmet and lowered his face guard. Training his restless gaze on the stands he searched for Bella as he cantered up to start the match.

CHAPTER TWO

BELLA hated him. Nero Caracas had almost single-handedly annihilated the home team. Never mind that his three team-mates had played well, she held Nero directly responsible for trouncing the team whose ponies she had trained. She had one bittersweet moment when the prince, who was awarding the prizes that day, had named Misty pony of the match, but even that triumph was quickly smashed by the quick look Nero shot her—the look that said, *I'm having her. She's mine.* The look that had prompted Bella to flare back silently, *Over my dead body.*

Over your body, certainly, had been Nero's outra-geously confident response, which he had laced with a wolfish grin. And now she was being forced into his company in the evening too. The prince had invited all the players and their trainers to dinner at the castle. It was not the type of invitation Bella could easily refuse. And why should she? The opportunity to eat dinner with the prince, to see round the royal castle—was she going to let Nero Caracas stand in the way of that? It was a signal from the prince himself that her father's yard was back in favour. Jack Wheeler's name would be spoken again with pride. And, realistically, her chance of being seated next to Nero was zero, Bella reassured herself. Protocol was everything in royal circles and she was sure to be seated with her team.

'I hope you don't mind that I put you next to me,' the prince said, smiling warmly at Bella, 'and that you're not sitting with your team…?'

'Of course not, Sir, it's an honour,' Bella replied graciously, trying not to care who was sitting across the table from her on the other side of the prince. Or the fact that Nero seemed unusually chummy with their royal host.

'The captain of the winning team and the owner and trainer of the pony of the match—it seemed an inevitable pairing to me,' the prince confided in his usual laid-back manner.

'Indeed, Sir,' Bella agreed, coolly meeting Nero's amused stare. What was going on?

'Your Royal Highness is, as ever, a most perceptive man,' Nero drawled, raising one sweeping ebony brow as he connected with Bella's narrow-eyed stare.

Bella Wheeler in a dinner gown. This was an image he had toyed with on his way to the castle. He had thought she might free her shiny auburn hair from its cruel captivity and reveal the young body that lurked beneath her workmanlike clothes. Instead, she was trussed up in a gown her grandmother would have approved of, and her hair was more tightly dressed than he had ever seen it. Did she have to make a statement every time they met? If it went on like this, he fully expected her to be wearing a sandwich board on the next occasion, proclaiming: Look, Don't Touch.

'So, Bella,' the prince said, distracting him, 'I've been hearing good things about you—and not just as far as training polo ponies goes. I'm thinking more of your work with children,' he explained.

Bella blushed. She didn't like to make a song and dance about the work she undertook in her free time.

'Have you ever thought of expanding your scheme?' the prince pressed.

Bella noticed Nero appeared to be equally intent on her answer. 'My polo commitments don't allow for it, Sir—'

'But you do what you can, which is more than most people even attempt,' the prince went on. 'And I've been hearing some very good things about you—'

Bella answered this with a modest smile.

As the meal continued her tension relaxed. She was imagining things, Bella reassured herself. Nero sitting across the table had made her edgy. There was no plan afoot between Nero and the prince. Her royal host was always well briefed, and was not only genuinely interested in the people he met but was an excellent conversationalist. Her father had been invited to the castle in his heyday, but this was Bella's first time and she wasn't going to waste it fretting about the prince's fanciful seating plan that saw spinster-and-contented-with-her-lot Bella Wheeler seated across the table from the world's most desirable man. She could only hope Nero had got her message—*Butt out of my life, Caracas. You're not wanted here.*

But she did want him. She wanted Nero with an ache so bad she could only hope the prince, who was undoubtedly a man of the world, hadn't picked up on it. Nero was a force of nature, a man who could have any woman in the world. What if he suspected how she felt about him? How professional would Nero think her then?

He'd think her a naïve fool. And he wouldn't be that far out. Right now, she was feeling as if she'd been parachuted in from Little Town in Nowhere Land to a life of such pomp and privilege she had to pinch herself to prove she wasn't dreaming. Thank goodness she'd found a gown at the back of the wardrobe suitable for dinner—ten years out of date, but conservative, which was all that mattered. She didn't like to draw attention to herself, which was another reason she appeared cold.

She stiffened and held Nero's gaze as he looked at her for one long potent moment, then turned away when the prince began talking to him. It was an opportunity to soak everything in—all the life-sized oil paintings on the ruby silk walls. Stout kings and thin kings, with glittering swords and crowns bearing testament to their wealth and power. Happy women and sad women, wearing sumptuous gowns, some of whom were surrounded by strangely disaffected children staring off bleakly into an unknowable future. With a shiver, she dragged her gaze away and began to study the vaulted ceiling instead. On a ground of rich cobalt blue, this was lavishly decorated with rosy-cheeked cherubs and cotton wool clouds and, coming back down to earth again, there was more crystal and silver on a dinner table made magical by candlelight than she had ever seen before. There must have been fifty people sitting at the table with them, and it was longer than a bowling alley to accommodate that number. A mischievous smile played around her lips when the royal butler and his team of efficient footmen strode silently by—some wild child inside her wanted to dance a crazy quickstep after them down the jewel-coloured runners that marked out their transit through the hall.

She could act serene, but inside her there was a wild

child longing to get out. Nero was as relaxed in this setting as he was on the polo field. How elegant and confident he appeared, lounging back in his chair, chatting easily to the prince—as well he might. Rumour said Nero lived in considerable style on his *estancia* back home, where he ruled his estate like his own private fiefdom. And if he had been devastating in match clothes, he was off the scale tonight in a beautifully cut evening suit. The dark cloth moulded his powerful frame to perfection, while the crisp white shirt and steel-grey tie showed off his tan.

Damn! He was watching her. She turned her attention quickly to her plate. She was safer with her ponies than with all these men. Men were strong and could physically overwhelm her, and Nero Caracas was the strongest of them all. When you'd fought and lost as badly as she had, you never forgot—

Yet here she was, wrapping her lips around the tines of her fork as if she wanted him to look at her.

Must she court danger at every opportunity?

It must be the Nero effect. She was never so foolish, but just sitting across from him was enough to make her act differently—made her monitor how she held herself and how she ate. She had even taken to sipping her drink demurely!

Damn this to hell! She was a professional woman, not some impressionable teenager. Straightening up, she made a special effort to engage the prince in a topic of conversation which she knew he would appreciate, but even the prince seemed to be on Nero's side.

'I'm surprised you haven't made an offer for the pony of the match, Caracas,' the prince observed after a few minutes of conversation which had fallen well within the bounds of what Bella considered safe.

Bella tensed. Must everything come back to this?

'But I have,' Nero said mildly. 'I would love to own Misty, but Ms Wheeler seems to have her doubts—'

'Doubts?' The prince's eyebrows shot up as he turned to stare at Bella. 'Señor Caracas has an enviable *estancia* in Argentina, with the best living conditions for polo ponies I've seen anywhere in the world—'

'And still Ms Wheeler doubts me.' Nero's eyes were glinting with humour as he attempted to capture Bella's stony stare.

'You must reconsider, Ms Wheeler,' the prince insisted. 'Nero is the best rider in the world, and as such he should have access to the best ponies.'

Should he? By whose right?

Bella flashed a furious look across the table, only to be met by Nero's relaxed, sardonic stare. Her heart thundered—and not with anger. She could have coped with that more easily than this lust-fuelled desire to engage in combat with him. But the prince's message was unmistakable. If she was intransigent she would lose his favour and, as the prince was one of the foremost sponsors of the game, everything she had worked so hard to build could quickly turn to dust. 'Your Royal Highness.' She appeared to agree—even adding a meek dip of her head, but inside she was fuming. She would not be forced to sell her most cherished possession—and Nero Caracas could stop pulling the prince's strings. There must be a way out of this and she would find it.

But then Nero foiled her by mentioning a project close to her heart and now, it appeared, close to his. He planned to work with children who wouldn't normally have the opportunity to ride. She'd been doing that for years, and had seen the benefits first hand.

'I want them to experience the freedom of the pampas,' Nero was explaining to the prince, 'and discover what life is like on my *estancia* in Argentina.'

She would like to find out too, Bella thought wryly. But then her suspicions grew when it became clear that the prince and Nero had been in negotiations for some time over this proposed scheme—long enough for Nero to persuade the prince to be its patron.

'There are many similarities to your own work,' the prince observed, turning to include Bella in their discussion. 'Perhaps you remember, I mentioned the possibility of spreading your good work a little further earlier this evening?'

She'd been set up, Bella thought angrily, noting the spark of triumph in Nero's eyes. And since when was Argentina *a little further*? It was half a world away. She must have paled as the prince indicated that one of the hovering footmen should refill her water glass.

'Sir, I cannot think of leaving England—especially so close to Christmas.' She was clutching at straws— and had broken royal protocol by speaking to the prince before he invited her to do so, but the prince, sensing her distress, was at pains to make amends. 'But Christmas in Argentina is so beautiful and warm. I'm sure that your concerns in this country could be addressed, and Nero would ensure paid professionals were on hand to help you with the day-to-day running of the scheme in Argentina.'

Had this already been decided?

Bella had never found it so hard in her life to hold her tongue, but to interrupt the prince a second time would be an unforgivable breach of etiquette.

'I understand your concerns,' the prince assured her. 'There's so much paperwork when schemes such as this are set up, but I don't see you being involved in that. I see you taking more of a hands-on role, Bella—teaching the children to ride, and sharing your love of horses with them.'

'But, Sir—' Bella's eyes implored the prince to understand that she couldn't leave her yard. She worked every hour of every day to be the best. She even turned to Nero for help, but he merely raised a sardonic brow.

'There would be ample reward,' the prince said, as if this would make a difference.

Bella flinched with embarrassment. 'It isn't the money, Sir—'

'Pride is a great thing, Bella, but we all have to be practical,' the prince replied. 'Nero's gauchos have centuries of knowledge that working closely with horses has brought them, just as we do. There's nothing wrong with sharing that knowledge amongst friends, is there?' The prince stared at her intently.

What could she say without appearing mean-spirited? 'You're quite right, Sir,' she agreed, avoiding Nero's sardonic stare.

'And you could take Misty with you,' the prince added, warming to his theme. 'I'm sure Nero would have no objections?'

Was this a joke? Bella wondered as the two men exchanged a knowing glance. And now Nero's stare was heating her face, but she couldn't pretend the cash on offer wouldn't be useful—

So Nero had won.

Misty could only benefit by being ridden by the greatest polo player in the world, and riding high in the prince's approval meant the future of her stable yard was assured. 'This doesn't mean I would sell Misty to you,' she assured Nero.

As the prince exclaimed with disappointment on

Nero's behalf, Nero said smoothly, 'I don't think we need to worry about that yet.'

But some time she would need to worry, Bella interpreted, tensing even as the prince relaxed. She was up against the might of Nero Caracas with no one, not even the prince, to back her up. 'I couldn't leave my work here,' she said firmly.

The prince sat forward as Nero offered what must have sounded to him like a reassurance. 'I would send a team to take over what is already an established scheme,' Nero said with a relaxed shrug. 'They would handle all your outstanding commitments.'

Was she the only one who could see the glint of irony in Nero's eyes?

Apparently, Bella thought as the prince sighed with approval. 'We would be in this together, Bella,' the prince confirmed, tying the knot between them even tighter. 'All I'm asking from you is that you share your expertise in the setting up of a similar scheme in Argentina to the one you already run in England.'

How reasonable that sounded, Bella thought as the prince turned his kind-hearted gaze on her face. Nero might as well have hog-tied her and served her up on a silver platter. Had his penetrating stare also worked out that he scrambled her brain cells and made her stomach melt? Almost certainly, she thought as his ebony brow lifted.

'Well, what do you think, Bella?' the prince prompted gently.

'Could I have some time to think about this, Sir?'

His Royal Highness hesitated.

'Not too much time,' Nero cut in, apparently oblivious to the rules of royal etiquette when it came to getting his own way.

* * *

After dinner a recital was to be held in the Blue drawing room, with the chance for everyone to freshen up first.

Freshen up? Bella raged silently, checking her hair was still securely tied back in the gilt-framed mirror hanging on the wall of the unimaginably ornate restroom. After listening to the prince's well-intentioned suggestions on one side, and batting off Nero's sardonic sallies on the other, she felt like a tennis ball being swiped between the two, frayed a little around the edges, but still ready to bounce—right over Nero, preferably.

Conclusion?

Her carefully controlled life was rapidly spiralling out of control.

Taking one last look around at all the beautiful things in the restroom—dainty chairs with soft leaf-green covers and the comforting array of traditional organic scent bottles lined up on a crystal tray for visitors to sample—she had the strongest feeling that if Nero had anything to do with it, it would be some time before she would be making a return visit here.

In this same anxious mood she opened the door and managed to bump straight into him.

'Ill met by moonlight,' Nero murmured with amusement as Bella exclaimed with alarm.

Her breath echoed in the silence as she stared up at Nero's strong, tanned hand on the wall by her face. 'Excuse me, please—'

He didn't move.

'I said—'

'I heard what you said.'

'Then would you let me pass, please?' She would fight off the effects of that deceptively sleepy stare.

'What's your hurry, Bella?'

'We should be getting back to the recital...'

Nero hummed.

Bracing herself, she looked up. Moonlight was indeed bathing them both in a strange sapphire light as it poured in through one of the castle's many stained-glass windows. The effect was wonderful for Nero's dark skin and thick black hair—she guessed her own face was a watery blue and her red hair a strange shade of green. Heating up under Nero's amused scrutiny, she launched a counter-attack. 'What were you doing at dinner with the prince and all that talk of a scheme?'

'It wasn't talk, Bella—'

'And I suppose it wasn't a ruse to make me sell Misty to you, either?'

'The scheme will continue, with or without your help, Bella.'

In his severe formal clothes, in this most refined of settings, Nero Caracas looked like a dark angel and more dangerous than ever. 'You led the prince to think I might sell Misty—and that my compliance with the scheme was a given.'

Nero's lips pressed down in a most attractive way. 'There's no mystery,' he said with a shrug. 'I offered to pay whatever price you ask for the pony. I doubt you'll find anyone who will match my offer.'

Or match Nero's compelling aura, or his physical strength, Bella thought, fighting off the seductive effect. It was impossible to be this close to Nero Caracas without feeling something, she reasoned, willing her voice to remain steady. 'I told you once—and this is the last time—Misty isn't for sale.'

'And what if the prince wants to buy her?'

Stunned by the idea, Bella gasped.

'Don't tell me that thought hasn't occurred to you,'

Nero murmured in his lazy South American drawl. 'And if the prince does want your mare, how can you refuse him?' Nero gave her a moment to soak this up, before adding dryly, 'Perhaps I can save the situation for you.'

Bella's eyes narrowed. 'What would it cost me?'

'Oh, come now, Bella. You know Misty would be happier with me than the prince.'

Check. And mate. Nero had cut the legs from under her. Forget the threat he posed in the personal sense—polo ponies lived to play the game and Misty adored the high-powered cut and thrust of the international arena. It was common knowledge that the prince had practically retired from the game, which meant Misty would hardly be played at all, whereas as one of Nero's pampered ponies, Misty would get every opportunity to indulge the passion the small mare lived for.

'Having doubts?' Nero prompted, pouncing on her hesitation.

'None,' she lied. 'I only wish you had some scruples.'

Nero laughed. Throwing back his head, he revealed the long, firm column of his throat. 'Your innocence is touching, Bella.' Dipping his head, he stared her in the eyes to drive the point home. 'I have no scruples when it comes to the game.'

Which game?

In the heat of the moment, she grabbed his arm. 'Just keep the prince out of this.' Feeling the heat and muscle beneath her hand, she quickly released her grip. Inhaling sharply, she shook herself round. Nero was an experienced man. You didn't come up against him without getting burned. This was all a game to him and if she had any sense she'd put some much needed space between them...

Nero's hand slammed against the wall at the side of her face.

'Get out of my way,' Bella raged with shock, green eyes blazing.

'So I am right,' Nero murmured, standing back.

'Right about what?' she said angrily, thoroughly discomfited.

'There is fire beneath that ice of yours,' Nero murmured.

Bella inhaled sharply as Nero stroked back a strand of her hair that had escaped its stern captivity. 'You can stop congratulating yourself on your perception,' she said coldly. 'It doesn't seem to have helped you where Misty is concerned.'

Nero's mouth curved disconcertingly. 'You seem very sure of that, Bella.'

'I am.' Her voice was shaking, but in some strange way she was enjoying this. Nero made her feel alive. She should thank him for goading her.

'Temper, temper,' Nero murmured, reading her.

She stood aloof, but they were still so close she could feel his heat warming her, and his spicy scent invading her senses and making her dizzy. Nero was enjoying this too, Bella realised with a rush of concern and excitement mixed.

And have you chosen to overlook that small thing called consequences?

How she hated her inner voice for intruding at a time like this, but she couldn't ignore it. Her fighting spirit might have made a comeback, but her ability to trust a man still had a long way to go.

CHAPTER THREE

THE corridor was silent until the sound of doors closing made them both turn. 'Oh, dear,' Nero observed dryly, 'it appears we've missed the recital.'

'And what will the prince have to say about that?' Bella murmured defiantly.

Nero sighed in response but didn't look a bit repentant. 'It seems we're both in trouble.'

More than he could know, Bella thought, brewing up a storm.

Nero lounged back against the wall with footmen playing silent sentry as he waited for the music to end. The moment the doors were opened again, the prince summoned them both over.

She might as well give up now, Bella thought as the prince said how happy it made him to indulge a friend. She had just smiled her thanks when the prince made it clear that friend was Nero. 'As you know, I have agreed to be the patron of Nero's charity,' the prince confided in her, 'but as I have so many calls on my time I would like you, Bella, to represent me.'

'Me, Sir?' Of course she was surprised but, crucially, the prince had taken the decision about going to Argentina out of her hands.

'I can't think of anyone better qualified,' he continued.

'You are the best trainer I know, Bella. And when the polo season comes to an end, what better use of your time could there be than introducing more young people to the joys of riding? See what you can do over there, Bella—what you can both do,' the prince added, gazing at Bella and Nero in turn. 'Though I should warn you, Bella, that when you leave the northern hemisphere behind and experience the very different world you are going to, you might want to stay there. Passions run high on the pampas—isn't that so, Caracas?'

'Exactly so, Your Royal Highness.' Nero's amused gaze switched to Bella.

'I know you'll enjoy the teaching, Bella,' the prince continued, turning serious again. 'And if you would do this one thing for me, I would feel I was still there, in some way. I'm afraid I can't spare anyone from my own staff. But who knows the relationship between man and horse better than you?' he added persuasively. 'It will mean you spending quite some time in Argentina, Bella, but I feel certain you will enjoy that as much as I did.'

How could she refuse now?

By taking in the triumph in Nero's eyes, possibly? Bella thought tensely. Or the amused tug at the corner of his mouth? How she wished she could snatch some reason out of the air why she couldn't go, but she couldn't afford to risk offending the prince. There was no escape, she concluded. 'I would consider it a great honour to assist you in any way I can, Sir.'

'Excellent. I'm glad that's settled,' the prince said, beaming. 'And now… If you will both excuse me?'

'Of course.' At last she could look at Nero. His expression was exactly what she had expected. And she hoped hers left Nero in no doubt that she would do this, but only because the prince had asked her. Working as an adviser for Nero's charitable scheme was a privilege; she was too polite to even think of the word to describe working alongside a man who challenged every sensible boundary she had ever put in place.

'You'll be my guest, of course,' Nero explained, all business now his triumph was in the bag. 'Working and living on the pampas will be very different to anything you are used to here, but I am confident that in time you will grow to love it.'

In time? Bella swallowed deep. There were so many undertones to that apparently innocent statement she could only be glad the well-meaning prince hadn't stayed to hear them. 'I wouldn't be able to stay very long…'

'But long enough for the project to be established. The children need you, Bella.'

'As does my yard and my horses. I have my own scheme, Nero.'

He checked her at every turn. 'You'd break your word to the prince?'

'Had you already decided this plan between the two of you? Was my agreement to the prince's proposal merely a formality?'

Nero smiled faintly. 'You're so suspicious, Bella.'

'With good reason, I think,' she flashed.

'I will hold myself personally responsible for maintaining the high standards you have set at your yard in the UK. As I told both you and the prince, I will send my most trusted team to ensure you have nothing to worry about—financially, or otherwise.'

Was he serious? The systems she had set in place to take care of things should she be incapacitated by illness, or be taken out of the picture in some other way, would ensure the yard ran smoothly. If she chose to do this, it was Nero she was worried about, working in close proximity to him being the major problem. 'I have made enough money to keep everything ticking over nicely, thank you. I don't need any help from you!'

'Your reputation does you much credit, Bella,' Nero snapped. 'It seems you are your father's daughter, after all.'

Bella blenched. 'What's that supposed to mean?'

Nero's powerful shoulders eased in a shrug. 'You can't make a decision and stick to it.'

'How dare you—'

'How dare I speak the truth?' Nero's eyes drilled into her. 'If you break your word as easily as this, Bella Wheeler, I'm not sure I want you as part of my scheme.'

For a moment she didn't trust herself to speak. Nero had blatantly manipulated her, but if she lost her temper and blackened her father's memory even more she would never forgive herself. Taking a deep steadying breath, she buried her pride. 'You give me your word that my work in England wouldn't suffer?'

'I do,' Nero assured her in a clipped voice.

'And my visit to Argentina would be conditional on coming home as soon as the scheme is set up.'

'I can't imagine why I would want you to stay beyond that.'

Her heart beat with outrage. Nero really knew how to cut her with words, she realised, smiling prettily for the prince as Nero escorted her out of the royal presence.

'This is a win-win situation, Bella,' Nero insisted as they strolled across the room. 'I'm surprised you can't see it.'

'How do you reach that conclusion?'

'The prince secures you as his representative. My

project secures your experience. And you get to keep your pony.'

'In spite of your scare tactics, my ownership of Misty has never been in doubt. So what do you get out of it?' Bella demanded suspiciously.

'I get to keep Misty on my yard—and even ride her—if you will allow me to?'

Nero's tongue was firmly planted in his cheek, Bella suspected. And his face was close enough to make her lips tingle. 'Do you really need my permission?' she countered. And would she be able to resist seeing the world's best polo player mounted on the best pony? Nero's laughing eyes and the curve of his sensuous mouth reflected his confidence that this would be the case.

'Most important of all, Bella, the children benefit,' Nero said, turning serious.

And that was the one thing she couldn't argue with. 'Believe me, your project is the only reason I'm saying yes to Argentina.'

'But of course,' Nero agreed smoothly. 'What other reason could there be for a respectable woman to visit my *estancia*?'

'I can't imagine,' Bella said frostily, smiling her thanks as a royal footman opened the outer doors for them.

'And where will you go now?' Nero asked her as a driver brought his ink-black four-wheel-drive up to the foot of the steps for him.

'Back to the stables for one last check on the horses.'

'As I'm going there myself, why don't I give you a lift?'

'I prefer to walk, thank you.'

'In an evening dress?'

'It's a pleasant evening, and I need the fresh air.'

'Well, if you're sure?'

'I am.' Her mind was still whirling with the fact that she had agreed of her own free will to walk into the lion's den—and not here on familiar turf, but Argentina, and the wild, untamed pampas, where she would be staying on Nero's *estancia*. She needed some fresh air to come to terms with that alone—lots of it.

'Then good night,' Nero murmured, his eyes glittering with triumph. 'I'll see you tomorrow when we will firm up your travel arrangements.'

Life had suddenly become very interesting, Nero reflected as he gunned the engine and drove away from the castle. Word had it that Isabella Wheeler lived in an ivory tower whose walls had never been breached, but he'd caught flashes of internal fires raging out of control. She reminded him of one of his spirited mares. They took their time to trust and were always looking for trouble, but that was because they had lost the freedom of the pampas, something they would never forget. What had Bella Wheeler lost that caused her such torment? Rumour said there was some mystery surrounding her. He could confirm that. Bella said one thing and her eyes, the mirror of Bella's soul, said something different. She was lying by omission. She was hiding something big.

Bella's outwardly contained manner intrigued him almost as much as her unnaturally well-groomed appearance irritated him. It wasn't often he met a woman who had her own life, her own successful career and wasn't looking for anything material from him. Far from it, Nero reflected wryly. If he had to categorise Bella after getting to know her a little better, it would still be under the heading: Ice Maiden. He had never met a woman who went all out to make herself as unobtainable and as aloof as she could and, the irony was, Bella didn't realise what a desirable prize that made her. He'd seen the way men looked at her as they dreamed of loosening her tight-fitting breeches. He knew how he felt about her. And, judging by the way Bella responded to him, she wasn't exactly immune to him either.

He wanted her. She wanted him. There should have been a very easy solution, but there wasn't, and he was going to find out why.

When she had satisfied herself that everything at the stables was as it should be, Bella's thoughts turned to her grooms. Some of them were very young and she felt responsible for them. Hearing that a couple of the girls hadn't returned to the small bed and breakfast where Bella had rented them rooms, she set out to look for them. She knew exactly where they would be. After the match a large, luxurious nightclub had set up camp in a marquee in the grounds. It was *the* place to be, the girls had assured her. Bella had seen pictures on the news and could understand their excitement. The huge white tent was decorated like something out of *Arabian Nights* with exotic silken drapes in a variety of jewel colours and dramatic water features shooting plumes of glittering spray into the air. A dance floor had been erected in the middle of the tent and one of the top DJs had been booked to keep the excitement of the polo match alive until dawn.

She was only halfway across the field when the bass beat started pounding through her. She was really out of her comfort zone. Even before the prince's invitation, she had refused the young grooms' invitation to join them. She had made all sorts of excuses—she was too old, too boring—and had laughed when they had protested she was neither. It was never easy to mix business with pleasure, even had she wanted to, but like an old mother hen, she was determined to make sure her girls were safe tonight.

She was off to a good start, having the right credentials, apparently. A member of the security staff recognised her and showed her straight in through the VIP entrance. The noise was amazing and there was such a crowd it was a while before she spotted the girls, by which time she had been sucked deep into the throng and men were speaking to her, offering her drinks and wanting to dance with her. She was here for business purposes, she told them frostily, tilting her chin at a determined angle as she headed for the girls.

The heat was overwhelming inside the tent after the chill night air. What with the press of people, the noise, the screams of laughter, the relentless beat, the flash of chandeliers and the glittering, garish splendour of it all, it was no wonder she was disorientated to begin with. Shaking off the faint sense of danger approaching, she pressed on, determined not to leave until she knew the girls had arranged to get home safely.

'Bella!' they exclaimed the moment they caught sight of her.

Before she knew it, she was on the dance floor.

'Meet…'

She didn't hear the rest—there were too many names and far too many new faces. She smiled and jigged around a bit, trying to string a few steps together on a heavily overpopulated dance floor on which there was hardly room to move, let alone dance. And she felt silly in her strait-laced dinner gown amongst so many cool young girls.

'Are you sure you're all okay?' she asked, drawing one of them aside. 'Have you made plans for later, or shall I call a taxi for you?'

'My brother's here,' the girl explained, angling her chin towards a tall, good-looking youth. 'No worries, Bella. Woo-hoo! Enjoy yourself!' And, grabbing hold of Bella's wrist, the girl dragged her back onto the dance floor.

And why not? Bella reasoned, glancing round. Everyone was here for a good time, and one dance wouldn't hurt. She didn't want to be a killjoy, and there was such an air of celebration it felt great to be part of it. There was certainly nothing to be concerned about—even if that persistent prickle down her spine refused to go away.

'Come on—you can't go now. You've only just arrived,' the girls insisted, gathering round Bella, who was still glancing anxiously over her shoulder, hardly knowing what she was looking for. They formed a circle round her so she couldn't escape, which made her laugh, and soon she was dancing again and everyone was shooting their arms in the air. After some persuasion, Bella did too. It was fun. It felt good to let go. Her hair tumbled down and swung around her shoulders. She tossed it back, making no attempt to tidy herself for once. She was just happy to lose her inhibitions—happy to lose herself in the music, and the moment.

Until it all came crashing down.

So this was where Miss Bluestocking hung out when she wasn't preaching death to desire and all-natural female responses. Those responses were only curbed when he was around, it seemed. Her glorious hair was flying free, and was as spectacular as he had always imagined it would be, and she was dancing with all the abandon he had suspected she might possess—a fact that wasn't lost on the men around her, though Bella appeared to be oblivious to the interest she was arousing.

The crowd parted like the Red Sea as he strode up to her. He stopped in the centre of the dance floor in front of the one person oblivious to his approach. Currently gyrating with her eyes closed and her hands reaching for the sky, the so-called Ice Maiden was mouthing lyrics to the raunchy track and grinding her hips in time to the beat with extremely un-maidenly relish. 'What the hell are you doing here?' he rapped for the sheer pleasure of seeing the shock in her eyes.

'Nero!'

'Yes, Nero,' he confirmed. 'So this is why you refused my offer of a lift.'

She pretended not to understand him, and was pleasingly flushed and unsettled as she smoothed back her hair. He showed her no mercy. Instead, he tugged her into his arms.

'What are you doing?' she demanded, struggling to find her severe face as their bodies brushed and finally connected.

'Oh, I'm sorry,' he mocked as she let out a shocked breath. 'I didn't realise you had come here to lead a temperance rally. I thought you were dancing...'

She manoeuvred herself so their lower bodies were no longer touching. 'You don't understand—'

'Oh, I think I do,' Nero argued, drawing her close again as the uptempo track segued into a slower number. 'I understand things such as this very well.'

'I mean you don't understand me,' she said, going as stiff as a board. 'This isn't what it seems—'

'This is exactly what it seems,' he argued.

'I'm only here to…'

'Check out the ponies?' he reminded her in a deceptively mild tone.

'I'm here to check up on my girls,' Bella argued hotly. 'Not that it's any business of yours what I choose to do with my free time.'

'Not yet it isn't.'

Nero's powerful hands were on her arm and on her waist, making it hard to think straight. And he was radically changed. No more the suave aristocrat in an impeccably tailored suit, Nero had found time to change his clothes and in a tight-fitting top and well-worn jeans that sculpted his hard, toned muscles it was no wonder the crowds had parted for him. He looked like an invading warrior. His shoulders were massive. His biceps were ripped. His thick, inky-black hair tumbled over his brow, while his sharp black stubble seemed more piratical than ever, giving him the appearance of some brigand on a raid. Worse—he had caught her off guard, obliterating her carefully constructed image for the sake of one reckless dance.

'So why are you here?' she demanded, determined to turn the tables on him. 'Looking for entertainment, Nero?'

'I was looking for you,' he fired back. 'I expected to find you at the stables so we could discuss your travel plans for tomorrow. Imagine my surprise when one of the stable lads told me where you'd gone.' As one inky brow rose it coincided with a move that brought them into even closer contact. 'I wouldn't have missed this for the world,' he murmured as she gasped. 'Imagine my surprise at finding Miss Butter-Wouldn't-Melt in Sodom and Gomorrah.'

'I was dancing with my friends!'

Nero shot a glance around at the men staring open-mouthed at Bella. 'Really?' He guessed none of them had seen Bella Wheeler breaking free before. The flickering light played into his hands, giving everything a hellish glow. Flashing and reflecting off the glitter balls hanging from the ceiling, the coloured lights made the mass of dancing figures seem contorted as if they were taking part in some primitive orgiastic rite. This was as far removed from the hushed sanctuary of the stable yard as it was possible to imagine. 'I would never have guessed this was your scene,' he murmured, twisting the knife. 'I understood you preferred an innocent stroll in the clean night air.'

He loved the way she writhed in his arms. She even balled her tiny hand into a fist, but thought better of using it on him, and gradually, in spite of all her best efforts, the stiffness seeped out of her and she softened in his arms.

'That's better,' he commented as she responded to the persuasive beat.

'Don't think I'm dancing with you because I want to.'

'Of course you aren't,' he agreed, soothing her as they moved to the music. There were only two things a man and woman could do to a rhythm when they were as close as this, and dancing was step one.

She couldn't have been more humiliated. Of all the things to happen, Nero discovering her midbellow in the middle of a raunchy song... How often did she let herself go?

Try never.

And that cringing feeling she got when some man she didn't know touched her—where was that? Nero felt amazing, not that she was touching him unnecessarily.

And then the music quietened and faded, and she waited for him to release her...

Was he going to kiss her?

Nero was staring down as if he might. They were alone in the middle of a packed dance floor. Closing her eyes, she drew in a shaking breath. Nero dipped his head...

The wait went on too long.

'See you tomorrow, Bella.'

She was left standing in confusion. Nero had walked off. People were staring at her.

With as little fuss as possible, she left the floor, making sure she took a different route. He was playing games with her, and she had no one to blame but herself. She could have brought that encounter to an end at any time. Why on earth hadn't she?

CHAPTER FOUR

IT WAS dawn when Nero rang the next morning. Bella was already at the stables. It had nothing to do with a restless night; this was her usual routine. 'Yes?' she said coolly. Answering the phone was easier than facing him.

'Travel plans,' Nero said briskly in the same no-nonsense tone.

'I'm listening.' And with some relief, she realised. After last night, she wouldn't have been surprised if Nero had left the country without another word.

The conversation that followed never strayed from the point, with Nero doing most of the talking. Bella was a highly respected professional, but Nero was the owner of countless polo ponies as well as being a top international player, so their respective positions in the game put him firmly in the driving seat. 'You will travel with me to Argentina,' he informed her. 'The horses will follow later when I'm satisfied everything is ready for them.'

Before she could ask if she would have any part to play in this, Nero went on to say that he would wind down in Buenos Aires before travelling to his *estancia*, which would give Bella chance to recover from the flight.

What form would Nero's wind-down take? And how much did she hate herself for wondering if she would even see him in Buenos Aires? She was still brooding about it when she ate breakfast with a group of red-eyed grooms.

It was ridiculous to care. This was business, Bella told herself firmly as she paid the bill and checked out of the small bed and breakfast hotel where she and the grooms had been staying. And she could hardly ask Nero what his intentions were—unless she wanted to appear desperate, of course.

Nero had been all male disapproval last night, but a spark had flared between them. She had acted cool at the castle, only for him to discover her dancing the night away, apparently surrounded by men. He had chosen not to notice the girlfriends dancing with her. Nero hadn't seen anything beyond the heat of the night, the throb of the music and the fact that everyone but him was in the same abandoned state. Nero would keep his word and honour their business arrangement, but he wouldn't forget. That pride of his would never allow it.

As she walked up the steps of Nero's private jet, Bella felt she was leaving everything certain behind and entering a world far beyond the scope of her imagination. There was a uniformed flight attendant to show her round while Nero joined his copilot in the cockpit. Everything in the interior of the plane was of the best— thick cream carpets, pale leather armchairs, just like a topclass hotel. Señor Caracas had his own private suite, the attendant explained, but Bella could take her pick from any of the other four options on board. She was still reeling from this information when the attendant added that Señor Caracas would meet her for breakfast the next morning as this was an overnight flight, and that in the meantime if she needed anything at all she only had to call him.

Was Nero avoiding her? Thinking back to her wild abandonment the previous evening, Bella went hot with embarrassment. It was so unlike her to expose herself like that—to become the butt of speculation.

But she'd done nothing wrong, Bella told herself firmly. Meanwhile, she should enjoy this. Her bedroom was small, but beautifully fitted with polished wood and a comfortable-looking bed dressed with crisp white linen. Thanking the attendant as he put her small suitcase down on the soft wool carpet, she vowed to put last night behind her and start again. This was just a short and fascinating interlude, after which she would return to her old life and Nero would carry on with his as if they'd never met.

And on that prescription she spent a restless night, tossing and turning, and waking long before the steward had arranged to call her. Having showered and dressed neatly in jeans and a long-sleeved top, she went to find breakfast. Nero was already lounging at the table in the salon, also dressed casually, his damp hair suggesting he was fresh from the shower. He greeted her politely above the hum of the engines and put down his newspaper.

Beyond that…nothing.

Nero was aloof, but knowing, Bella thought, flashing him a covert glance as she gave her order to the hovering steward. He had perfected the art of saying nothing and conveying too much, she thought, feeling her cheeks blaze red. Nero knew she had wanted him the other night—knew she had expected him to kiss her. It hadn't changed his mind about their business arrangement, but it had changed Nero's manner towards her, giving him more the upper hand than ever. He had formed an opinion about her and, mistaken though that opinion was, she didn't feel like offering an explanation for having fun in her free time.

He stared at Bella thoughtfully. She was discreetly dressed with her hair scraped back from a make-up-less face. Did she think he was going to throw her to the floor and have his evil way with her? After the other night he'd got her message loud and clear, as if he needed a reminder. As if he was interested.

But he was interested, which gave him a problem. And the more Bella played him, the more interested he became.

Bella wasn't sure what to expect when the plane landed. She had thought plenty about their destination and had bought every travel guide going, though beyond describing the pampas she had learned nothing about Nero's ranch. She couldn't wait to see where he lived and realised it was a measure of the power Nero wielded, as well as the security surrounding him, that only wild speculation could be rooted out regarding the lifestyle of one of the world's most private men. The first surprise came when they landed. She hadn't really thought about the practicalities of leaving a private jet. It proved to be a real eye-opener. Her passport was checked on board and a sleek black saloon was waiting for them on the tarmac at the foot of the steps.

The first thing Bella noticed as she exited the aircraft was how beautifully warm it was after the chill of London. The sky was blue and as she walked down the steps the spicy scent of Argentina blotted out the sickly fumes of aviation fuel. Waving the chauffeur away, Nero opened the passenger door for her and as soon as she was comfortably settled inside he shut the door and walked round to the driver's side. The checkpoint at the exit might not have existed. The bar was quickly raised and they were waved on their way by a guard who saluted them as if they were royalty. Which, in many ways, Nero was, Bella reflected, shooting him a sideways glance. The king of polo was looking more than usually splendid this morning and, in spite of all her strongest warnings to self, she felt her senses roar. Dark and dangerous described Nero to a T and who didn't like to dabble their toes in danger from time to time…?

'Are you going to buckle your seat belt any time soon?'

Nero's voice was rough and husky and she nearly jumped out of her seat to be caught in the middle of some rather raunchy thoughts about him. She buckled up without reply and gave herself a telling off. Better she leave the danger to those sophisticated women—the 'stick chicks' as they were known in polo circles. Far better for someone like her to stay in the stables with the ponies, Bella concluded wryly.

They were soon speeding down the highway towards the city. It was impossible to relax in such a confined space with Nero sitting beside her. He broke the silence only once to explain that he had booked her into a hotel in the centre of Buenos Aires where she would have the chance to recover from the thirteen-hour flight.

'Thank you,' she said, falling silent again. Nero didn't want conversation, and she didn't have the first clue how to start one with him. Without their mutual interest in horses or the kindly prince to prompt her, she was lost.

Nero drove as he played polo, at speed and with

confidence, and there was enough testosterone bouncing round the small cabin of his high-powered car to
drown in. If a man could increase his sex appeal just
to taunt her, then that was exactly what Nero had done.
The relentless march of his sharp black stubble had won
the razor war and he looked every bit the tough, tanned
lover, wearing jeans that clung to his hard-muscled
thighs and sleeves rolled back on his casual shirt to
expose his powerful forearms.

What would working for him be like? Bella wondered. Everything in Nero's life was his way or no way.
It remained to be seen what would happen when he
worked alongside a woman who felt exactly the same
way about her ponies.

As they drove on through the unprepossessing out-
skirts of the city Bella's personal concerns shrank to
nothing in the shadow of the shanty town stalking the
highway. No wonder Nero wanted to share his good
fortune with youngsters who had so little. What she
was seeing now would make it easy to forget her personal feelings about Nero and throw everything she'd
got behind his scheme.

'It's known as Villa 31,' he said, noticing her interest
in the depressing sprawl. 'It's been here fifty years or
more, and it's still growing. No point dwelling on it,' he
added. 'We have to *do* something.'

Narrowing his eyes, Nero stared ahead as they sped
past the chaotic urbanisation, but he was seeing a lot
more than the road, Bella guessed.

It was late afternoon when they arrived in the centre
of Buenos Aires, by which time shadows were falling
over the graceful buildings. This was another side of the
coin, Bella thought, as she peered out of the car window
at the romantic soul of Argentina. No wonder Buenos

Aires was known as the Paris of South America, or that Nero was so proud of his homeland. The sun was still putting up a good fight and as it sank had turned the ancient stone a rosy pink, though as the day waned she thought Nero seemed to grow in force and intent like a creature of the night. It was as if this return to his homeland had stirred fresh passion in him, and as it swirled around them in the confined space of the car it infected Bella too. She had never felt so acutely aware, or so excited by the prospect of what lay ahead of her.

Nero had joined the heavy traffic on a grand twelve-lane boulevard with a soaring monument at the end of it. 'El Obelisco,' he explained, his glance sparking a lightning flash down Bella's spine. 'The tapering obelisk celebrates four hundred years of the founding of our capital city. There is so much beauty here,' he murmured, resting his stubble-shaded chin on one arm as he waited for the traffic to move. 'As you will learn, Bella,' he said, turning to lavish a longer look into her eyes, 'Argentina is a country of huge contrasts and monumental passions.'

The passion she already knew about, but the pride in Nero's voice made Bella envy his sense of belonging. She felt her body thrill at his attention, and it was all she could do to stop her imagination taking over. The most she could reasonably hope for, she told herself sensibly, was that this trip heralded a fresh start between them. If they could put their differences behind them she could experience something of the diversity of Argentina with Nero as her guide.

'Everything is on such a vast scale,' she commented, dragging her stare away from the huge phallic monument. It was a relief to let her gaze linger on what appeared to be a glorious fairy-tale chateau lifted straight out of some lush green valley in France.

'That's the French embassy,' Nero explained. 'It's a fantastic example of Belle Epoque architecture, don't you think?'

Bella nodded, relieved to be talking about something innocent after the way her thoughts had been turning.

'It was built in the golden age before the First World War when the world was still innocent,' Nero mused.

Bella turned to keep the magical building in sight. 'And yet it looks so right here—'

'Where nothing is innocent,' Nero murmured.

Silence hung between them for a while and then it became clear they were leaving the centre behind and entering an area with a uniquely quaint beat rather than a city atmosphere. 'I thought you might like the cobbled streets and Bohemian atmosphere...'

Was Nero teasing her? It was never easy to tell. Whatever his motive, it was clear he had booked the strait-laced Ice Maiden into one of the hottest areas of the city. The narrow streets were still crowded with pedestrians and there was a wide choice of clubs and bars and interesting little shops.

'I hope you approve, Bella?'

'I'm certainly intrigued.' She was longing to explore.

'Here we are.' Nero drew the vehicle to a halt outside a small chic boutique hotel. 'I chose this particular hotel because it's far enough away from the action for you to get some sleep, but close enough, should you wish to sample it,' he added with a touch of irony.

'I'll be far too busy sleeping,' she countered, turning away from Nero's mocking stare.

She was acutely aware of his strong hands on the

wheel and the determined jut of his chin. Nero was in control for now and she had to step up to the plate or go home, and she had no intention of going anywhere until her job was done. Nero might think he could control every woman as he controlled his polo ponies, but not this woman. And with that silent pep talk over Bella felt a lot more confident. 'Thank you for the lift.'

Leaning across, Nero stopped her opening the door, which was enough in itself to blank her mind of all her fragile resolutions. 'Allow me,' he said, staring into her eyes.

Oh, that long, confident Latin stare—when would she ever learn to deal with it? Bella wondered as Nero opened the door for her. She hadn't missed the ironic twist of his mouth. Nero thought she was easy meat and simply acting tough. He was right about one of those—she was acting. She was in a strange country with a man she hardly knew, and she felt vulnerable. Only when they reached Nero's *estancia* and she was working with her horses in a setting she understood would she be totally at ease again.

She stood for a moment on the cobbles in the warm gardenia-scented air. She just wanted to soak everything in. She could hear music playing in the distance. This was even better than the Buenos Aires she had dreamed about. And was that really a couple dancing in the street?

'Tango—the lifeblood of Buenos Aires,' Nero informed her in his deep, husky voice.

Bella's heart was beating off the scale—surely Nero must hear it? She hadn't even realised he'd come to stand so close beside her. Sensibly, she moved away. She had to keep all her wits about her on this trip. This was only page one of her Argentinian adventure, and the book promised to be as exciting and surprising as the country Nero called home.

CHAPTER FIVE

DETERMINED to maintain her cool, Bella fixed her gaze on the hotel entrance as she started up the steps. The polished wooden door had black wrought-iron decoration of a type that seemed to be fashionable in the area. Nero was definitely right about the area's appeal. The cobbled streets and colonial buildings, coupled with Bohemian chic *and* the tango, gave it an irresistible charm.

She gasped as Nero held her back.

'Don't you want to stay and watch the dancers for a moment?'

Night was closing fast and shadows elongated the dancing couple into lean, languorous shapes. They were dancing without inhibition—not for an audience, but for themselves. They were unaware that they had been captured in the spotlight of a street lamp in the middle of the city. Staring intently into each other's faces, the dancers inhabited their own erotic world of fierce stares and abrupt movements, finishing in sinuous reconciliation. The tango was the dance of love, Bella realised.

'There is a *milonga*, a neighbourhood dance hall where people go to dance tango—quite famous, actually—just across the street,' Nero explained, bringing Bella back down to earth again. 'That couple will almost certainly be practising for their performance tonight.'

'I'd love to see them dance,' Bella murmured, transfixed by their skill. The man was resting the woman over his arm so that her hair almost brushed the pavement, and the woman was slim and lithe, and dressed for a night of dancing such as Bella couldn't even begin to imagine—and had certainly never experienced.

And was never likely to, she told herself sensibly, but how she envied the woman her confidence and her style. She was wearing the highest stiletto heels and the sheerest black tights with a fine seam up the back, and her dress was the merest whisper of black silk that flicked and clung to her toned, tanned body. The man was taller, but he too was lean and strong. He guided and directed his partner in a way that seemed to have no answer to it until she snapped her legs around him, and that spoke of another truth—that a woman with the right sort of confidence could tame any man.

Right, Bella thought as she watched them, but not this woman, not me. And not this man, she reflected, stealing a glance at Nero. No wonder she was a stranger to this type of dancing. Pulling herself round, she turned to follow the porter into the hotel.

'Do you want to go there later?'

She stopped dead, completely dumbfounded by Nero's question. She felt a shiver of awareness streak down her back. She must have misheard him, surely? 'I'm sorry?' She turned to face him.

'Perhaps you're too tired to go out tonight?' Nero suggested dryly.

Nero was inviting her to join him at the tango club? The mocking challenge in his voice sent warning tingles down her spine. But wasn't this what she had wanted?

On the simplest level she longed to see something of Buenos Aires while she had the chance. Let's not even go near the complicated level, Bella concluded. But hadn't Nero said that tango was the lifeblood of the city? 'As long as I don't have to dance,' she said, feeling happy now she had put a condition on accepting his invitation.

'Don't worry,' he said dryly, 'I've seen you dance.'

A curl of excitement unfurled inside her as Nero met her stare. 'I'll pick you up at ten,' he said.

Now what had she done? Bella wondered as Nero got back into his car and roared away. One thing was sure; she was playing a far more sophisticated game than she was used to.

Up in her hotel room, with its state portrait of a very beautiful and glamorous Eva Peron smiling down, Bella's problems were mounting. She had packed three sets of riding gear for this trip, an unflattering old-fashioned swimming costume that covered up far more than it revealed, a matching cover-up, a pair of shorts, some work clothes, jeans, sneakers, boots, a pile of T-shirts, some serviceable underwear and a couple of sweaters. At the very last minute she had added a neat pencil skirt with a pair of chunky-heeled shoes, a tailored blouse and jacket, just in case she needed to attend a business meeting during her visit. Tango costume, it was not.

Though as she wouldn't be dancing...

She definitely wouldn't be dancing, Bella told herself firmly, remembering how it had felt to be held in Nero's arms at the polo party. And, as strictly speaking this was a business outing with her boss, the pencil skirt would be perfect. Tying her hair back neatly, she told her heart to stop behaving so erratically and, with a final check in the mirror, she drew a deep breath and left the room.

Nero was leaning against the wall at the foot of the stairs. Surrounded by an adoring crowd, he was signing autographs. Yet another reminder that she was out of her depth here. Thank goodness for her sensible business outfit. There was no danger she could be mistaken for one of Nero's girlfriends looking like this. In fact, she should be able to reach the front door without anyone noticing her—

'Bella?'

Wrong. Nero was at her elbow. Or, rather, she was at his. He was so much taller than she was. He was like a solid wall of muscle protecting her from his fans, all of whom seemed intent on getting a piece of him. But all he had to do was speak a few words in his own language and with a collective sigh of understanding the crowd fell back.

'What did you say to them?' Bella asked, impressed.

'I told them you were here so you could learn to dance—' Nero's powerful shoulders eased into a typical Latin shrug. 'I explained that you come from a place where dancing is practically unheard of, and that this is a mercy mission on my part. They understood completely.'

I bet they did, Bella thought. She tilted her chin as Nero held the door for her and walked past him with what she sincerely hoped was a businesslike expression on her face—in the manner of a woman whose intention was to do anything but dance her way into danger tonight.

The tango club was situated on the top floor of an old building. Vast and echoey, the white-flagged floors had turned grey with age and the tiled staircase was of the same vintage, but the people hadn't come to admire the architecture. They were being drawn upstairs by the heady pulse of music, which floated down from an open doorway on the upper landing.

Bella was soon to discover that the whole of the attic space had been transformed into a dance hall. The air was warm and sultry, and the room was lit by candlelight which gave it a golden shadowy hue. The scent of wax melting was added to the faint overlay of perfume and warm clean bodies—and something else…something heady and alluring, which Bella flatly refused to identify as emotion, let alone passion.

Wooden chairs surrounded tables covered with welcoming red-and-white cloths—though no one seemed to be eating as far as Bella could tell—they all were too intent on watching the tango demonstration. The room was packed and hushed. A couple was about to start. A table was quickly found for Bella and Nero, who murmured something in Spanish to a waiter before ushering her ahead of him. She was so drawn to the upcoming performance she almost stumbled—and would have done if Nero hadn't steadied her. 'Sit, Bella,' he prompted.

She sank down on the hard wooden chair, tingling from his touch. This next couple seemed to be the one everyone had been waiting for—and this wasn't the glitzy entertainment Bella had seen on TV back home, but something earthy and sensual, and unashamedly erotic. The moment the accordionist began to play she was drawn into another world. The couple on the dance floor held each other's gaze intently as they moved with feline languor to the steady beat of the music—though this could change in a heel tap into something fierce and aggressive. As the rhythm rose in a climactic wave Bella realised that these dramatic changes from slumbering passion to outright conflict and back again to soothing gestures were exactly what the spectators had come to see. There was no doubt the woman gave as good as she got—pushing her partner away with a blistering glare, only for him to snatch her back again.

This was how her life could be, Bella reflected whimsically, leaning her chin on the heel of her hand. Instead of safe and bland, she could change it in an instant to risk and danger and attack—

Nero returned her to reality with a jolt, asking her what she'd like to drink. 'Water, please.' She didn't trust herself with anything stronger.

How far out of her comfort zone was she now? Bella thought as the performance heated up. If there was one thing she had already learned in Argentina, it was that the tango was the vertical expression of horizontal desire, and she'd have preferred something a touch safer for her first outing with the boss.

Her boss...

It could be worse, she reflected dryly, taking him in. Nero had dressed for the evening in slim black trousers that complemented his incredible physique. His powerful shoulders tapered to his narrow waist, which was cinched by a leather belt. His shoes were black and highly polished, and his shirt was white and crisp—

And he was dressed for dancing, Bella realised with a sudden blaze of panic. Nero was an athlete—one of the world's top athletes. And the tango at this level couldn't be attempted by anyone who didn't enjoy peak fitness. 'Do you dance?' she said weakly as the crashing finale and riotous applause brought the display they'd been watching to a close.

'I love to dance,' Nero assured her, putting down his

glass of wine. 'I love anything where I have to use my body.'

She didn't doubt it, Bella thought, swallowing deep as one of the startlingly beautiful young girls in the club sashayed towards their table. How could she compete with this? Was that why Nero had brought her here? To humiliate her? Was this Nero's revenge for not allowing him to buy Misty?

She was clutching her glass so hard she would break it if she wasn't careful, Bella realised. Then some demon got into her and, throwing caution to the wind, she sprang to her feet. 'I'll dance,' she said wildly, only to find her voice blasting through a momentary silence.

People stared at her. The young girl stared at her. How ridiculous she must seem in her office clothes when everyone else around her was dressed…well, not for the office.

'Bella?'

Tall and imposing, Nero was holding out his hand to her. The music was thrumming with an almost irresistible beat. She did a quick inventory. Her skirt had a slit up the back and everything that should be covered was covered—

And she was nothing if not game. She hadn't come to Argentina to be pushed around, or to be pushed into the shadows. Adopting the typical haughty stare of a female tango dancer, she tilted her chin as a challenge to Nero to follow her to the dance floor.

'Are you sure about this?' he murmured.

The sexy sibilant syllables tickled her ear as she whispered back, 'Absolutely certain—'

She wasn't sure about anything—her own sanity was most in question. But she had excelled in Scottish country dancing at her all-girls school.

'In that case…'

Snatching her to him, Nero managed in the shadows of the dimly lit club to look more saturnine and menacing than he ever had. She tilted her chin a little higher to acknowledge the round of somewhat hesitant applause. 'You'd better lead,' she conceded.

'Oh, I'll lead,' Nero assured her.

'And take it slowly, please—'

'I will,' he promised, sounding amused.

And then her palm was flat against Nero's strong, warm hand and a whole universe of new feelings opened up to her. It would pass, Bella told herself confidently. She was only going to dance with him. What was the worst that could happen? She could make a fool of herself. Something told her that Nero would never allow that to happen. And for just once in her life she wanted to unselfconsciously do something she had watched and admired others do. 'I just have to make sure I don't tread on your feet,' she said awkwardly as they waited for the music to begin.

'Relax,' Nero murmured. 'Just imagine that you're a pony I am breaking in.'

What? 'I'd rather imagine I'm a woman and you're a man who is very kindly teaching me an unfamiliar dance.'

'Oh, I think you'll be familiar with this dance,' Nero murmured.

Bella gulped. She had to be the only person here who wasn't familiar with the dance of love. But how could she not respond to Nero's hand in the small of her back, or the insistent pressure of his thigh? He could be so subtle and so persuasive and, though she wasn't doing anything clever like flicking her leg through his, she was moving to the music. Nero's control of the dance was absolute, and yet his control was so light she could understand why his polo ponies were so responsive to him. Was it wrong to want a little more pressure? Was it really possible that Nero had such an incredible level of sensitivity, or such a sense of rhythm, and such an acute insight into what pleased her most?

'You dance well,' he said as a smattering of applause greeted their first experiment. 'You have a natural flair.'

Only thanks to him, she thought.

'And now let's try and put a little more passion into it. Look at me, Bella. Look at me as if you hate me.'

At least something was easy.

'That's good. Now soften a little…entice me…'

She could do that too—but not too much. A brush from Nero's body was like a lightning bolt to her system. No one was required to weld themselves to their teacher, Bella reassured herself. She would call upon her underused acting skills instead. Raising a brow, she stared at Nero beneath her eyelashes. Lifting her ribcage, she adopted a more dramatic pose—a move that got her a little more applause.

'Easy,' Nero growled in her ear when she attempted to lead him. 'This is only your first lesson.'

'Then there will have to be many more,' she assured him, growing in confidence and feeling invincible as more couples joined them on the floor.

Perhaps the right word was invisible…

Whatever. She was beginning to think the ability to dance the tango was a prerequisite for living in Argentina. 'From what I've seen tonight, I'm going to need those lessons,' she admitted.

'You certainly will,' Nero agreed. 'And I'll be sure to find someone good to teach you.'

As Bella went stiff and pulled away Nero drew her back again, inch by steady inch. And, yes, she should put an end to this, but why, when Nero kept each move so slow and deliberate and she could easily follow him, and he never once made her feel that he was mocking her, or that he would step over the all-important boundary from stylised dancing into something more threatening and real? He always maintained a space between them and, though some people undoubtedly found tango as intoxicating as sex, she had realised it was the promise of sex rather than the act itself, and as a woman who didn't like admitting how inexperienced she was, that held enormous appeal. Unlike the frenzied bouncing in the marquee at the polo ground, this was dance as art.

Nero loosened his grip when the music faded and led Bella back to their table. 'You're full of surprises, Bella Wheeler,' he said, narrowing his eyes as he gave her a considering look. Raising his hand, he called the waiter over to bring them another drink.

'Just some more water, please.' She had more surprises locked away inside her than Nero could possibly guess at, and she was going to keep a clear head while she was in Argentina to make sure she kept it that way.

CHAPTER SIX

KEEPING a clear head guaranteed Bella an early night. Nero delivered her to the door of her hotel and, with a brisk nod, bid her good night. Put him out of your head, she told herself next morning. She was ready to explore.

The Sunday traffic was every bit as crazy as when she had arrived, but she welcomed the noise and bustle of a new day, thinking this was the most exhilarating introduction to a city as fascinating as Buenos Aires that she could possibly have. And she certainly wasn't going to sit in her hotel room wondering what Nero was doing. He had said he would call for her at eleven that morning to take her to his *estancia*. Where he was or what he did before then was Nero's business.

And she didn't care a jot.

Liar, Bella thought as she left the hotel. But she was determined to make the most of her short stay in one of the world's most vibrant and beautiful cities. This was just one of the places Nero called home, and she was curious to explore it. Buenos Aires was full of personality and charm, the staff in the hotel had assured her. Everywhere she went she would find *porteños*, as the residents of Buenos Aires were called, performing the tango on the streets. Crowds gathered, music played, and dancers dressed for the occasion would entertain you, they told her with a smile.

She didn't have to look far before she discovered a small square at the end of the street where an impromptu dance floor had been created simply by laying board down on the cobbles. The sun was warm, the sky was blue, the setting was exquisite and she joined the crowd to watch. Colourful gardens surrounded her and the central fountain in the tiny square provided a pleasant overlay to the music. A small white rococo church with steeples like plump figs added to the charm of the setting. She was really in South America now, Bella thought, feeling excited and rather cosmopolitan. Shading her eyes, she watched the dancers and soon she was lost in their skill, and in the music, and was hardly aware that someone had walked up behind her.

'How easy it would be to relieve you of this,' a husky male voice very close to her ear said disapprovingly.

'Nero!' Her heart lurched violently. So much for playing it cool. The heat of the dance was all around them—most of it in her cheeks when Nero held up the wallet he had taken from her handbag.

'Your handbag was open,' he explained. 'Lucky for you the hotel told me where I could find you. I hope you're packed and ready to leave?'

'Of course.' She was thrown immediately from carefree tourist into awkward sort-of-employee, and had to move quickly on from that mind-set to professional woman whose only purpose in being in Argentina was to do a worthwhile job for the prince of her country. She held out her hand for the wallet and Nero gave it to her. Stuffing it back into her shoulder bag, she fastened the catch securely. 'Do you make a habit of this?' she demanded.

'Do you make a habit of leaving your wits behind when you travel?' Nero countered.

They stared at each other. The dance between them had begun. Tango must be catching, Bella thought dryly. 'Shall we?' she said, keen to break eye contact.

'By all means.'

She turned for the hotel. That husky Argentine accent was the sexiest in the world, she decided as she led the way.

And she'd soon get used to Nero's voice and let it wash over her, Bella told herself firmly, quickening her step. But however prim she tried to act, Buenos Aires worked against her. There was too much passion here—too many dancers expressing their feelings on this Sunday morning, swirling, spinning, legs flicking, arms raised at acute angles—men in spats, women dropping as if into a dead faint in their partners' arms, only to revive so they could continue the fight. It was exhausting just watching them.

'Tango gets into your blood,' Nero commented when they reached the steps of Bella's hotel.

Then she must be sure not to let it get into her own blood, Bella thought. 'I'll just ask the porter for my suitcase. I left it ready in the lobby when I checked out.'

'Your case has already been taken to the airport.'

'The airport?' Bella's throat dried. Was Nero sending her home? Were her services no longer required?

'I take it you won't mind being my only passenger?' he demanded.

She must have looked at him blankly. 'In the jet,' he prompted.

'You'll be flying a jet to the *estancia*?' she confirmed.

'Yes. Is something wrong with that?'

'No, of course not.' Didn't everyone have a selection of private jets from which to choose?

The cockpit of Nero's executive jet was yet another confined space in which Bella was forced to sit too close to Nero. Of course, she could have sat in the back where there were comfortable leather seats, and entertainment as well as refreshments on tap, but she had given way to a childish urge to sit next to the pilot.

And taste a little of that danger she was growing so fond of?

She had always been fascinated by the concept of flight, Bella argued primly with her inner voice.

And fascinated by Nero.

Why pretend? She had an overriding desire to sit next to Nero.

He checked the buckles on her seat belt and helped her to fit the headphones securely. 'Okay?'

Her senses soared to answer him before she could. He smiled deep into her eyes. Nero saw everything, Bella realised, turning quickly to stare out of the window. By the time he had completed his pre-flight checks she could hardly breathe for arousal. He was totally in control, and his self-assurance filled her with confidence—and not just as to how well Nero would fly a jet.

'There's no need to be nervous,' he said, turning to look at her.

'I'm not nervous,' she protested, consciously relaxing her grip on the seat. Just sitting next to him was making her nervous. Going to Nero's *estancia*, where the only way out was by private plane, or goodness knew how long a road trip, was nothing short of insanity.

'Don't look so worried, Bella; I'll take care of you.'

That was what she was afraid of. 'The only thing

wrong with me,' she said as Nero lined up the jet for take-off, 'is that I like to be in control. Sitting in the copilot's seat doesn't suit me.'

'But it suits me very well,' Nero assured her, breaking off to acknowledge instructions from the control tower. Having been given the all-clear, he opened the throttle and released the brake and in seconds, or so it seemed, the small jet rocketed into the clear blue sky.

There was no turning back now, Bella thought as the jet soared through the first bank of cloud.

After a couple of hours the clouds parted to reveal a very different world from the towering skyscrapers and sprawling urbanisations of Buenos Aires. Nero's private airstrip was little more than a thin stripe of bleached earth on what seemed to be an endless carpet of green and russet and gold, stretching towards a horizon where misty mountains clawed at the cobalt sky with jagged fingers.

The Pampas. Bella's heart leapt with an intoxicating mixture of excitement and fear. The thought of riding here—of living here—with so much space, and so close to nature—

'Wait until you breathe the air,' Nero murmured.

Pollution-free and as heady as the most refined wine, Bella guessed.

'Here,' Nero told her as he banked the jet steeply. 'Take a look out of the side window and you'll see the *estancia*.'

Bella gasped as the g-force hit her.

'Nervous now?' Nero suggested with a wicked grin.

'Not at all,' Bella lied as the jet levelled off.

'You'll need steady nerves while you're working here. Life is tough on the pampas, Bella.'

'I'm not here for easy,' she told him frankly. 'I'm here to do the best job I can.' Her gaze turned to the hundreds of horses on the ground below.

'We had a lot of foals born this year.'

'Incredible,' Bella murmured. Everyone knew Nero was a wealthy man, but this was a polo establishment on an unimaginable scale.

'I'll fly you over the house before we land.'

Her stomach flipped as the plane dropped lower. The house Nero was referring to was an elegant colonial-style building the size of a small town, and now they were only a hundred feet or so above it she could see the long shaded verandas and a formal garden as vast as a park. There was even a polo field at one end of the cultivated grounds, with a stand and clubhouse, while in the central courtyard of the main building a fountain spurted diamond plumes into the air. Behind the house there was a glistening lake with a fabulous sandy beach and one—no, two swimming pools...

'One is for the horses,' Nero said when he saw her looking. 'We use it for treatment and for strengthening exercises, though we ride in the lake for preference—'

Bella exclaimed with pleasure, but then her usual common sense kicked in. What on earth had she been thinking when she had agreed to this? Nero's vast estate was like a country in its own right. She would be as isolated here as if she had been shipwrecked with him and they were stranded on a desert island with the ocean surrounding them. Unless she could find some way to ignore the electricity that constantly sparked between them, this could turn into a very tense and challenging stay.

Nero landed the jet skilfully with scarcely a bump. As he slowed to a halt and cut the engines Bella's concerns gave way to excitement. 'Oh, just look at that,' she exclaimed as she stared out across the miles of rolling grass. 'I can't wait to get out there and smell the air.'

'Feel the sun, and ride the horses,' Nero added with matching enthusiasm. 'It's beautiful, isn't it?'

When the door of the jet swung open Bella was greeted by a gust of warm, fragrant air. She was so excited she didn't even shrug off Nero's steadying hand when he helped her down the steps. There was always that small adjustment from sitting and floating to stepping out onto terra firma—add her eagerness to that and she was like a wild pony who, for that moment at least, was glad of Nero's reassuring presence. A wind had kicked up, blowing her hair about, and the ground was dusty and hard beneath her feet, but the warmth of her welcome was in no doubt at all.

'This is Ignacio,' Nero explained, introducing an elderly man standing by the utility vehicle waiting to take them to the ranch. 'My estate manager and right-hand man.'

Now she really was on the pampas, Bella thought, feeling a thrill of excitement as the elderly man stepped forward to shake her hand. She took in the slouched hat and red bandana, the voluminous trousers worn with leather chaps to protect the gaucho's legs from the constant friction of riding a horse. 'Welcome to Estancia Caracas,' he said in heavily accented English, bowing briefly over Bella's hand.

'*Buenas tardes*—good afternoon,' Bella replied, feeling more than welcome.

'We have heard many good things about your work with the English horses,' Ignacio added graciously.

'And battled the proof of it on the polo field,' Nero said as both men laughed.

'You're too kind. Your work with horses is second to none in Argentina.' Nero's estate manager had skin like beaten leather and was as wrinkled as a turtle, but his raisin-black eyes were full of kindness and warmth, and his handshake was firm. 'I'm so pleased to meet you, Ignacio. *Mucho gusto.*'

Ignacio grunted appreciatively at Bella's attempt to speak his language and said something in rapid Spanish to Nero that elicited a noncommittal hum.

Whether Nero was pleased or not by her clumsy effort, she had made one friend, Bella thought, judging by the warmth in the elderly gaucho's eyes as he invited her to sit in the vehicle for the short drive to the house.

She found everything thrilling, even the bumpy ride during which Ignacio pointed out the colourful ducks flying in arrow formation against the flawless blue sky, and then Nero spotted one of the giant hares native to the pampas as it bounced across the road. 'Look, Bella,' he said, grabbing hold of her arm in his excitement.

That touch was most thrilling of all, she thought, and the sights were pretty spectacular. And now Nero's powerful arm was resting across the seat in front of her. The only decoration he wore was a steel wristwatch that could probably tell their position in relation to the moon, but his sheer physical presence was what overwhelmed her.

'Good, huh?'

She jumped alert as he prompted her. 'Amazing,' she murmured, staring into his eyes. This time she had to force her stubborn gaze outside the vehicle.

They entered Estancia Caracas through an arched

entrance that reminded Bella of old cowboy films where the gates loomed large and impressive in what was otherwise a barren landscape. A long, well-groomed drive led the way to the sprawling hacienda—though this was a hacienda with a capital H—far larger and better kept than seemed humanly possible in such a wild and remote area, she decided as Ignacio turned into a cobbled courtyard the size of a football pitch.

'Wow,' Bella murmured. Nero's home was seriously fabulous.

They got out and she paused for a moment. The breeze was tickling the leaves on the eucalyptus trees and the only other sound was the distant whinnying of a horse. The courtyard was full of flowers—vivid cascades tumbling down the walls and draping in lush swags over the balconies. 'You must find it so hard to leave here,' she murmured.

'And so good to come back,' Nero agreed. 'Shall we?'

'Yes, of course.' The walls of the hacienda were painted in a muted shade of chalky terracotta, while the smooth cobbles beneath her feet were a deeper shade of golden red. Everything looked so warm and welcoming beneath the cobalt sky.

'Is this not what you had expected?' Nero demanded as Bella exclaimed with pleasure as she trailed her fingertips across some clusters of blossom.

Of such a hard, rugged man? 'No,' she admitted. 'I don't know what I expected, really.'

'So what do you think now?'

'That you have mastered the art of living in harmony with your surroundings,' she said honestly.

Nero seemed pleased by this analysis and introduced Bella to María, his cook and housekeeper, and María's sister, Concepcion, both of whom were waiting to greet him outside the door. The older ladies' faces were wreathed in smiles. They were so obviously delighted to see him Bella could only conclude Nero must have been an engaging child.

Perhaps she was being a little unfair to him, Bella conceded as the women bustled ahead, turning constantly to check that Nero hadn't left them again. The large hallway was paved in fabulous terracotta marble, softened by cinnamon-coloured rugs. The walls, painted a warm cream, were hung with antique mirrors and pictures. Probably family heirlooms, Bella guessed, apart from a painting of a wild horse, which was more recent and drew her attention immediately.

'Do you like it?' Nero asked, noticing her interest.

'I love it,' she enthused. Gadamus was an American artist noted for his freestyle technique with an airbrush and there was nothing cosy about this picture. There was nothing cosy about her life any longer, Bella thought as she glanced at Nero.

'So, what do you like about it?' he probed.

'The brutal realism,' she said, holding his gaze.

'You're drawn to danger and risk?' Nero suggested.

'It appears so,' Bella agreed coolly. She refused to be over-faced by all this quiet money, or by a man of such power and charisma.

'We'd better not keep María and Concepcion waiting,' Nero pointed out, making her a mocking bow.

They understood each other completely, Bella thought, though her confidence in handling Nero was short-lived. His touch on her arm shot the breath from her lungs as he held the door for her and they traded the shady lobby for an interior courtyard.

She quickly recovered to take in the peaceful haven

where the only disturbance was the sound of water gushing in the fountain to a background of birdsong. The air was scented with blossom, which reminded Bella that Christmas in Argentina was very different to the same season in England. The prince had warned her that she would be leaving the cold northern hemisphere for something very different. How right he was. This was another world altogether...

'You have a beautiful home, Nero.' And she was allowing herself to invest far too much interest and emotion.

The interior of the house made it even harder for Bella to disengage her feelings. There was a grand hall with a sweeping staircase, and the lake they had flown over was the focus of all the main rooms. From the windows of each elegant salon she could see beautifully tended lawns sweeping away to a golden beach and, in the far distance, snow-capped mountains.

'Do you approve?' Nero demanded dryly.

'I've never seen anything like it,' Bella admitted. 'But I'm here to work,' she managed in a firmer tone.

'Of course.'

Nero held the door for her and as she passed in front of him he made her feel so very small and vulnerable. Why must every part of her respond to him so urgently? Her mind must remain set on business, she told herself firmly.

'This is my den,' Nero explained, showing her into a smaller wood-panelled room. 'But you must make yourself at home here.'

Bella felt her smile must be little short of incredulous. Making herself at home here would take a little longer than she intended to spend in Argentina. 'I don't know how you can ever bear to leave,' she exclaimed impulsively.

'That's only because you haven't seen my place in Buenos Aires yet,' Nero informed her dryly.

And was never likely to, she thought. Hey ho.

CHAPTER SEVEN

'You must be hungry,' Nero suggested, leading the way to the kitchen. 'I know I am,' he said.

Nero's lips were pressing down so attractively she would have followed him anywhere, Bella mused wryly.

The kitchen took up a large part of the ground floor, and was another design triumph. State-of-the-art appliances sat comfortably next to well-worn settles and pieces of riding equipment. And, judging by the boots, gloves and polo helmet resting on a small side table next to an easy chair, this was the heart of the home and Nero's preferred space. The seat and the back of the chair wore the imprint of his body, Bella noticed, dragging her gaze away.

'What do you think?' Nero asked.

Censored. Dreams she could have, but she wasn't sharing them with him. 'Something smells good,' she said, inhaling appreciatively. And such smells they were—aromatic broth steaming busily on top of the old range cooker, the scent of freshly baked bread and ground coffee. Bella's mouth was watering by the time María and Concepcion had invited them to sit at the large scrubbed table.

'Perhaps you would like María to show you to your

bedroom first—so you can freshen up before you eat?' Nero suggested. 'Whenever you're ready, come down, we'll eat and then I'll take you on a tour of the stables.'

'Perfect. Though the bunkhouse would suit me fine,' Bella protested as María led the way into the hall.

'The bunkhouse?' Nero raised an amused brow. 'I'm not sure the gauchos would take too kindly to you moving in. And how could I deny María and Concepcion the pleasure of your sunny nature?' he added dryly.

Was she really such a stuck-up, starchy old maid? She must appear so, Bella realised. If only she could learn how to relax without giving Nero the wrong idea.

Her bedroom was beautiful, full of the scent of flowers freshly picked from the garden and deliciously feminine. She would never have indulged herself to this extent with all the lace and frills and flowers at home. It proved to be another occasion when she had to drag herself away.

She hadn't realised how hungry she was and devoured the delicious meal María placed in front of her. When she finally sat back with a contented sigh she noticed Nero watching her.

'Ms Wheeler?' he said formally, standing to hold her chair. 'Would you care to see the stables now?'

She flashed him a quick smile. 'Thank you, Señor Caracas. I would love to see the stables…'

The prince hadn't exaggerated. Nero's stables were unlike anything she'd seen before—six-star accommodation for horses with amenities second to none. For a moment Bella almost lost her confidence. Everything she was used to back home was so low-key compared to this. Nero's yard was the Bugatti Veyron Super Sport to her banged-up Mini of a polo yard.

But she produced great horses, Bella reminded herself.

It was Nero who shook her out of these concerns when he reminded her that the youngsters would be arriving soon, and that Ignacio wanted to show Bella the ponies he thought suitable for novices. These were retired ponies who couldn't take too much weight and whose exercise regime had been drastically reduced. 'As long as we make sure their mouths can't be dragged—and I have a cure for that,' Bella said, explaining her process with the reins to Nero. Before she knew it, she was right back where she belonged, chatting easily to him about horses. This was one area at least in which there were no tensions between them.

The stables were cleaner than many hotel rooms Bella had stayed in; sweet-smelling hay was banked high and her imagination took flight in the shadowy stall. 'We'd better get on,' she said abruptly, giving Nero one of her tight-lipped smiles.

'Why so tense, Bella?'

'I'd like to see the clinic,' she said, concerned that Nero could read her mind.

He shrugged. 'As you wish.'

Nero's shadow fell over her as he opened the stable door. He made her feel so small and feminine, which was something quite new for Bella. And she would ignore it, she determined.

And that was easy, Bella thought wryly as Nero led the way across the yard. He had changed out of his casual travel clothes into close-fitting breeches, which he was wearing with a deep maroon polo top. The contrast of colours against Nero's tanned skin made for a compelling picture. The wide spread of his shoulders and the hard, tanned chest just visible at the neck of his top didn't hurt either. And she wouldn't have been looking at his breeches if she hadn't been admiring his fabulous knee-length black leather boots. She noted with concern than the placket at the front of his breeches appeared to be under some considerable strain...

'This way,' Nero prompted.

'Of course,' she said, tipping her chin at a professional angle as she followed him.

'I have a polo match next week.'

'Next week?' So soon? And the children were arriving when?

She could cope. She would cope.

'Ignacio thought you would enjoy preparing the ponies with him.'

'I would,' Bella agreed, quickly burying her concerns. 'That's what I'm here for.' She thrilled at the challenge.

'I want the kids to get straight into it as soon as they arrive,' Nero explained, 'and this friendly match with a neighbouring *estancia* will be their first proper introduction to polo, so everything must go smoothly.'

'And it will.' She only had one concern left. Did Nero know the meaning of a *friendly* match? Somehow, Bella doubted it. 'A week isn't a lot of time to prepare the ponies.'

'My ponies are always ready.'

She didn't doubt it. Proud. Hard. Driven—didn't even begin to describe this man. Competition was everything to Nero and, just as she had suspected, this would be anything but a friendly match—and those ponies had better be ready.

It wasn't just the way Nero looked, it was the way he

moved, Bella reflected, allowing him to walk ahead of her so she could assess him like prime breeding stock. She might be the Ice Maiden, happily set on her spinster ways, but that was no curb on admiring a perfect male physique. She was a professional, wasn't she? Bella thought as Nero turned to flash a quick glance her way to make sure she was following. What else did she do all day at work if not stare thoughtfully at muscle and flesh to make sure the beast in question was in tip-top form and had the stamina to do what was required of it without injury? This beast was definitely at the peak of fitness, and Nero's stamina had never been in question.

'That was a heavy sigh,' Nero commented, hanging back to keep pace with her. 'Not tired already, I hope, Bella?'

'Not tired at all. In fact, I can't remember feeling quite so energised.'

'Excellent.' Nero's lips pressed down with approval. 'The pampas air is obviously good for you.'

Something was, Bella thought as her mouth formed the Ice Maiden line.

'This is the hospital and recovery block,' Nero explained as they approached a smart white building.

He held the door open and she walked in under his arm. Heat curled low inside her in a primitive response to Nero's size and virility. The untamed pampas had loosed something elemental inside her. It was just as well the facilities inside the clinic were exceptional and she could quickly become absorbed in these.

'We can carry out operations here if we have to,' Nero explained. 'Vets live on site. There is also a doctor and a nurse in residence to care for the two-legged members of the team. The distances are so vast here we can't rely on help reaching us in time.'

Wasn't that the truth? she thought.

'Bella?'

'Wonderful,' she said, refocusing. 'May I see the facilities for the children now?'

'I can assure you they will be well catered for.'

Bella met and held Nero's proud gaze. 'I wouldn't be doing my job if I left out one of the most crucial parts of it.'

'As you wish.'

Even Nero's back had something to say about her thoroughness. Nero was a fierce, passionate man to whom pride meant everything, and he didn't take kindly to having his establishment judged by anyone, especially her. But pride was important to Bella too, at least where doing the best job possible was concerned.

'I trust this meets with your approval?' he said, opening the door to the first wooden chalet.

How prim and boring he must think her, Bella realised as she took a look around. If she were a child staying here she would be in seventh heaven—there was even a view of the ponies grazing in the paddocks through the windows. 'It's wonderful.' She turned to find Nero with his arms braced either side of the doorway, displaying his formidable physique as he leaned into the room. 'Did you plan the finishing touches while we were in Buenos Aires?' she said, noticing the recent magazines and the latest teen films stacked by the TV.

'I had nothing better to do.'

Nero's tongue was firmly planted in his cheek, Bella suspected. 'What?' she demanded when he raised a brow. 'I didn't spend all my time in Buenos Aires learning to dance the tango...'

'How very noble of you, Bella. And how reassuring for me to know our evening out wasn't wasted.'

She groaned inwardly. What a dull companion he must think her. 'I'll take some shots for the prince,' she said, finding her phone.

'I trust your report will be favourable?'

'How could it not be when you've thought of everything—even fire extinguishers.'

'You won't need one,' Nero murmured under his breath.

The Ice Maiden had never regretted her tag more— and this time there was plenty of room for her to pass Nero at the door without touching him. He was standing well clear.

'Would you like to see the ponies we have chosen for you to look at?'

'I'd love to.'

'So you do trust our judgement?'

'Ignacio's reputation precedes him.'

'As does mine, I have no doubt,' Nero observed dryly as they walked along the dusty path together.

This time she thought it better to say nothing.

CHAPTER EIGHT

As BELLA had expected, Nero and Ignacio had judged the ponies perfectly. 'These will be a match made in heaven,' she said, 'and will give the kids loads of confidence.' She was conscious of Nero brooding at her side and wondered what was on his mind.

'We'd better go,' he said, pulling his booted foot from the fence rail. 'The first group of kids will be arriving soon, and I've no doubt you'll want to settle them in.'

'It's you they'll want to see,' Bella pointed out. Whether he chose to accept it or not, Nero was a national hero. 'It's no secret that half the kids we're expecting to join the scheme would have scoffed at the idea of leaving the city for the wilds of the pampas if there hadn't been a certain attraction named Nero Caracas waiting here for them.'

'Are you attempting to flatter me?' Nero laughed. 'I should warn you, I am immune to it.'

In the same way that familiarity bred contempt? Bella thought. 'I'm merely stating a fact.'

'Then allow me to reassure you,' Nero murmured as they walked back to the hacienda side by side, 'I'll be with you every step of the way.'

Oh, good, Bella thought wryly as her glance crashed into Nero's. 'I'm sure the children will appreciate that.'

'And you will too, I hope?'

The mocking note in Nero's voice hadn't escaped her. 'That goes without saying,' she said.

'Your wish is my command, Bella.'

And if she believed that then she was well on her way to becoming a doormat. Nero would tolerate her involvement at Estancia Caracas for the sake of his scheme and the prince's goodwill—and nothing more. She would have to work harder than she ever had in her life to make this work, Bella realised as Nero snapped his whip against his boots. At least she'd be too tired to dream about him at night. If brooding Nero intended to shadow her she would just have to act out a part—someone confident in her personal as well as her professional life—someone sophisticated who could handle Nero's high-powered sex appeal and take it all in her stride.

Someone else?

There was no one else. There was just Bella Wheeler, the Ice Maiden, and Nero Caracas, the Assassin. Oh, good.

They parted in the kitchen to shower and freshen up. When Nero came downstairs again it amused him to see María stuffing *empanadas*, the delicious little stuffed pastries, inside Bella's mouth as she crossed the kitchen on her way out, and pressing even more pastries into her hands as she tried to get through the door. Someone had made a friend.

'Sorry,' Bella garbled, chewing down a mouthful as he left the house to join her.

'Don't apologise,' he said, stealing a pastry from her hands. 'Hmm, delicious,' he agreed, smacking his hands together to get rid of the crumbs.

She risked a smile.

'What are you wearing?' he demanded.

'Dungarees—I thought, settling kids in, carrying cases...'

He shrugged.

'You don't agree?'

'There are others here who can carry cases. Wasn't it you who said we're the inspiration? And, as in this instance, I agree you're right, and so I dressed the part.' Nero ran a hand down his black polo shirt with the team emblem—The Assassin's skull and crossbones boldly embroidered in white on black over his heart. His hand moved on down his close-fitting breeches, tough riding boots and the knee protectors he customarily wore during a match. 'This is all about first appearances, you said—give the kids something to remember?'

'I see what you mean...' She frowned, but swiftly rallied. 'I suppose none of them would have a clue who you were if you were waiting for them wearing jeans.'

He met the innocent look with the faintest of smiles. 'You're probably right,' he agreed mildly.

'So, as I'm short of a Hammer House of Horrors polo shirt, what do you suggest I wear?' she asked.

Holding the concerned gaze, he put a curb on his amusement. 'What would you think if you were greeted by a woman in dungarees?'

Bella shrugged. 'The grooms were too busy caring for the horses to hang around waiting for my coach?' she suggested, reasoning that the grooms were all young—and, however scruffy they got in the course of their work, all attractive. The kids would only think an older woman in dungarees a poor substitute who probably knew nothing about horses, anyway.

'And?' Nero pressed, dipping his head to stare her in the eyes.

'The owners and trainers had better things to do?'

'And how would that make you feel?'

'Okay,' she agreed. 'You've made your point.'

'As you made yours,' Nero pointed out wryly.

He was right. If Bella had been one of the kids arriving on the coach she would like to think her arrival counted for something—enough, at least, for the people who ran the course to be waiting to greet her. 'I'll go and put something else on.'

Nero glanced at his watch. There was just enough time for Bella to change her clothes. He watched her return to the house, straight-backed, with a brisk stride. He anticipated the transformation with interest.

'Much better,' he approved when she cocked a brow before mutely running her hands down her neatly packaged frame.

Much, *much* better, he thought as his body responded with indecent enthusiasm to Bella's transformation. This was far better than dungarees, and a vast improvement on her working breeches. It was even better than Bella in a straight-laced evening dress.

'Would you like me to do a twirl?' she asked with a heavy dose of sarcasm.

'I've seen you dance, remember? So I know twirls aren't your strength.' He held her gaze. He loved holding her gaze. And so they stared at each other—staring into each other's eyes, neither one of them prepared to back down.

Until the sound of a coach approaching forced them both to glance away. But even as he stood ready to welcome the children he was keenly aware of the extremely attractive woman standing at his side dressed in no-nonsense breeches and a crisp white tailored shirt.

* * *

The children were settling in, but there was no time to relax. While his team of gauchos took the children through safety procedures and introduced them to the ponies, it was time for Nero and Bella to turn their thoughts towards the polo match. 'Let's get started, shall we?' he said, heading off towards the stables.

Bella pulled a wry face as she tucked a strand of rebellious hair back into position. 'I hope you don't live to regret involving me in this.'

He did too.

'Are you sure you're not going to find this too much? Teaching reckless kids and even wilder ponies?' He stared into her eyes, wanting to study Bella more deeply. He was a practical man. Sometimes lust intruded. Usually he would take a practical view of what was on offer—make his decision—yes or no, and then move on. Bella was too vulnerable for that. She might be acting the role but, like any actress, Bella's woman-of-the-world façade came off with the costume.

'I'm sure,' she said, meeting his gaze confidently. 'I have some experience of...coping.'

She spoke without emotion, and then he remembered Bella had three younger siblings—brothers, none of whom were interested in horses or their father's yard, and all of whom had gone on to university, thanks to Bella's riding boot up their backside. The children had lost their mother at an early age, and when their father had gone to pieces it had been left to Bella to set things on an even keel. There was more to this Ice Maiden than most people even guessed at and, remembering what he'd seen of her other side on the dance floor, he said, 'I hope you'll make time for your tango lessons. Or will they have to be put on hold for now?'

Her timing was perfect. There was a short pause,

and then, 'Why should they be put on hold?' she asked, 'Ignacio has promised to hone my technique, so the next time you and I hit the dance floor, I'll be ready for you.'

'Oh, will you?' he said.

So Ignacio was going to teach Bella the tango, was he? First María, and now Ignacio—what was happening here? 'You want to watch Ignacio,' he said, narrowing his eyes in mock suspicion. 'Many a good tune is played on an old fiddle.'

Bella laughed, letting herself go for the first time in a long time, but then she angled her chin to stare into his eyes. 'Are you jealous, Nero?'

He huffed and turned away.

'Could we have a drink before we start thinking about the polo match?' she asked, catching up with him in the yard.

'Water okay for you?'

'Perfect,' she said.

He led the way into the barn. Opening the door, he let it swing shut behind them. They were instantly enclosed in warm silence. Walking over to a sink in the corner, he filled a container with the crystal-clear water that flowed straight from the glacier via an underground stream to the hacienda. 'We'll take this with us,' he said, offering the container to Bella first.

She drank deeply and then handed it to him. He did the same. As he wiped the back of his hand across his mouth he caught her staring at him. His mouth curved with amusement as he read her thoughts. They had shared a drink from the same container. It was the closest their mouths had come to touching—up to now.

She was within touching distance of Nero. There was something magical about a hay barn. Perhaps it was the mountains of dried grass soaking up the sound, or the dust motes floating on sunbeams giving the impression of a shimmering golden veil between them. It was a soft—a ridiculously soft—frame, in which Nero appeared violently masculine.

'Bella?' he murmured.

'Could I have another drink?' She reached for the canister. Their fingers touched as Nero handed it to her and a bolt of electricity shot up her arm.

'We'd better fill it again before we leave,' he said as she lowered the container from her lips. Holding her gaze, he removed it from her hand and placed it on the side. She drew in a sharp breath as Nero's hands rested lightly on her arms.

'What are you frightened of, Bella?'

She couldn't look at him even though the temptation to let go just this once was overwhelming. 'I'm not frightened.'

'Prove it,' Nero said quietly, and behind his customary irony Bella sensed a deeper layer of concern.

'Shouldn't we be getting on?' She glanced across the honeyed space—the chasm between them and the door. Nero was like a sleeping tiger, breathing steadily and yet keenly aware at the same time. She had never played the mating game before, but she knew the signs. The look in Nero's eyes—the attractive tug at one corner of his mouth. Nero liked her. No. It was a lot more than that…

'Bella, Bella,' he murmured.

She swayed a little closer.

But something was wrong…something was out of sync. It felt as if she was edging along a tightrope with the promise of the most wonderful reward at the end of it with snapping sharks waiting in the waters below. At no point had Nero touched her—in fact, he had pulled back, and now one brow was raised in sardonic enquiry. 'What was that about?' he said.

Softening had been an insane lapse of judgement on her part—that was what it had been, Bella thought. She shared a professional relationship with Nero and that was all.

Until he dragged her close and rasped, 'You have no idea what you're playing with.' And, as she stared up at him in mute bewilderment, he added, 'I advise you very strongly to think before you act, Bella. You think you know me? You think you can play your schoolgirl games with me?'

'Don't worry,' she flashed, bouncing back onto the attack as she broke free. 'There's not the slightest chance I will ever play games with you.' And, when Nero laughed, she added, 'You're not as irresistible as you seem to think you are.' And that was meant to be her exit line, but Nero snatched her back again. 'Let go of me,' she warned him.

'You don't want this?' Nero smothered her cry of protest the most effective way he could. Brushing his lips across hers until the need poured out of her in whimpers of anger and frustrated tears, he took possession of her mouth in a fierce salty kiss.

Balling her hands into fists, she thrust them against his chest. She soon learned that fighting Nero was pointless. She should have hated him for this victory, but how could she when she wanted him, and when every encounter in the past was as nothing compared to this? The taste of him…the spice and scent of warm clean man…the feelings flooding through her veins…the heat pooling in her heart, her body, her senses…the need building up inside her…the urge to claim him as her mate.

When Nero kissed her the world and all its complications fell away. There was nothing left but sensation and the absolute conviction that this was right.

'*Dios*, Bella!' He thrust her away.

Shaken to the core, she was panting, while Nero towered over her, looking down as if he hated her. 'What if I was a different man, Bella? Don't you know what a dangerous game this is?'

'It's a game you're playing too,' she whipped back, hand across her mouth as if that could hide the proof of her arousal. She had to turn away to catch her breath before she could come back at him. Gripping the edge of the sink as if her life depended upon it, she drew a deep calming breath. Nero was right. They were both equally to blame for this. She had wanted him, but this was wrong. They were both wrong.

On the outside at least, she was utterly calm by the time she turned round again. 'We shouldn't keep Ignacio waiting,' she said coolly.

Nero opened the barn door and she walked through. And now it was back to business, Bella told herself firmly. She must forget this as if it had never happened. Or lose her credibility.

Her work provided the lifeline. The sound of churning water saved her. It distracted her and she exclaimed with interest when their route to the polo yard took them past the hydrotherapy spa. 'Can I take a closer look?'

'Of course.' Nero hung back while she went to watch the pony having its treatment. Rubber matting on the floor and side walls prevented accidental injury, and the spa stall was just large enough for the horse to feel safe as the healing salts in the chilly water bubbled around its legs. 'This is fantastic,' she commented.

'The low temperature increases the pony's circulation

and speeds up the curative process,' Nero explained, coming to stand beside her.

She breathed a sigh of relief. Thank goodness they had found something of interest in common that didn't put either her reputation or her heart at risk. 'I don't have anything like this in England.' She flashed a glance at Nero, and then remembered how things stood between them.

'I'm sure you'll find everything you need here, Bella.'

'I'm sure I will,' she said, determined to ignore the shiver of arousal that rippled down her spine.

CHAPTER NINE

AS PART of the final matching process between horse and rider for the upcoming polo game, Nero was mounted and ready to give a riding demonstration. This was primarily for Bella so he could show her each pony's paces and quirks, though the newly arrived youngsters from the city had been invited to watch too.

This was why they were here, Bella thought as she watched the rapt faces around her. Nero might look like a movie star, but they all knew he wasn't playing a role, and he was doing more than show the paces of each horse. He was making the kids hungry—making them aspire to do better—to be the best they could be, so they could make a difference in the world in which they lived. But for now, Nero could turn a polo pony on a sixpence. He could gallop, skid to a halt in a cloud of dust within inches of the fence and make them all scream. He could prompt a pony to weave and turn, back up, rear round and change direction constantly, without appearing to move a muscle. And he did all this with the nonchalance of a Sunday ride in the park.

Nero was cool—really cool. He wasn't just the master of the game or even the horse he happened to be riding. Nero was master of himself, and that was sexy. He was powerful, and yet he coaxed a wild animal to be part of a team, and to do that he had to be sensitive and almost primal in his understanding of the relationship between two living things—and almost preternaturally refined in the delicacy of the adjustments he made to draw differing responses from the horse. It didn't take much to start wondering how that sensitivity of his might translate in bed.

And she had to stop thinking like that right away. She joined in the applause when Nero cantered round the ring acknowledging the appreciation of his audience with one hand raised. Staring at his strong tanned hand and imagining how it would feel resting on her naked body—firm, yet light and intuitive when it came to dealing pleasure. She had to stop that too.

'Did you draw any conclusions?' Nero demanded, reining in his horse in front of her.

'Plenty,' Bella managed as her throat went suddenly dry.

'Good.' Slipping his feet out of the stirrups, Nero eased his powerful limbs. 'I look forward to hearing your comments when I've helped the boys take the ponies back.'

'Right.' She nodded as he wheeled the pony away, but she was still rather more drawn by his muscular thighs straining the seams of his breeches than by any conclusions she had made on the work front. 'Get real, Bella,' she muttered impatiently under her breath.

Nero and Ignacio received her comments with approving nods. At least she hadn't lost it where horses were concerned. But that didn't address the bigger problem, Bella mused as Nero started to walk off with Ignacio. Staying in the house with him meant she saw Nero every day. She couldn't afford to slip up again like she had in the barn. 'I'll see you later,' she called to the two men as she headed off in the opposite direction.

She could be happy here, Bella realised as she walked along the path between the paddocks and the warm breeze ruffled her hair. It was the type of life people dreamed of, with the added spice of Nero close by. Reaching the house, she was already anticipating the welcoming smiles from María and Concepcion. The warmth of family, she thought as she opened the kitchen door. Kicking off her boots, she lined them up on the mat. Walking across the room, she left her helmet and riding gloves where Nero left his. It was maybe the closest she'd come to him since their kiss...

Seeing her smile fade momentarily, the two beaming women hijacked her with a piece of chocolate cake. 'Mmm—delicious,' Bella exclaimed, biting deep.

'More,' the two women insisted, cutting her a second slice.

'I'll miss you both so much when I go home,' she told them both in halting Spanish whilst fending off their attempts to force-feed her. She'd tried to learn more of the language, wanting to get closer to the people she was living with. She had only been in Argentina a short time, but it had made a huge impression on her. It wasn't just the facilities here, or even the challenging ponies...

It must be something in the air, Bella decided wryly, sucking crumbs off her fingers as she headed for the door. Nero *and* the pampas? That was quite a combustible combination for anyone to handle...

So she'd leave it for someone with more relationship smarts than she had.

And now she was jealous of that unknown some-one.

She must remember not to let her feelings show, Bella

realised as María chased her to the door in an attempt
to feed her more reviving chocolate cake. Laughing and
holding up her hands in submission, she took the cake,
dropped a kiss on María's cheek and ran upstairs to her
bedroom.

Trailing her fingertips across the beautiful hand-
worked quilt, Bella's gaze was drawn as it had been the
first time she'd walked into the room, to an oil painting
over the fireplace. Bella's mother had been soft and
kind, but the woman in this portrait had Nero's fierce
stare and was dressed like a gaucho in men's clothes.
The only nod to femininity was the froth of chiffon at
her neck.

Bella lay on the bed, staring at the portrait. The strong
character of the woman in the painting blazed out at her.
That must have been one formidable lady, Bella thought,
taking in the determined set of the woman's jaw, the
unflinching gaze, and the line already cutting a cruel
furrow down one side of her full red lips. The likeness
to Nero was uncanny. And I bet she had a sardonic smile
too, Bella mused. The woman in the painting looked as
if she could cut any man down to size with either a whip
or her tongue. It pleased Bella to recognise the countryside in the background, though the *estancia* appeared
much smaller. No wonder the ranch had grown, she
thought, smiling as she took in the woman's planted fist
on top of the sturdy fencing. The portrait spoke volumes
about Nero's ancestry and why he was so attached to
the *estancia*. With people like that in his family, how
could he not be?

Nothing much had changed, Bella reflected as she
went to take a shower. Estancia Caracas might be huge
now and home to a very rich man, but Nero was as
much a warrior as the woman in the painting. Had no

softening influences touched him? What about his parents? Had they been written out of the picture? He never spoke about them. What sort of childhood had he had? And would she ever know?

It seemed unlikely, Bella thought as she soaped herself down. Nero wouldn't confide in her, and she could hardly question his staff.

One idyllic day melted into another, with Bella growing ever closer to Nero's staff until she felt like a real member of the team, and the youth scheme was going even better than she had dared to hope. Ignacio lightened everything, making her laugh and drip-feeding her information about Nero, as if the elderly gaucho wanted her to know what made his boss tick. The portrait in her bedroom was Nero's grandmother, he explained.

No surprise there, Bella thought dryly. She only had one regret left. She hardly saw Nero. They ate at different times, and he never seemed to be around when she was teaching. Whether he was too busy preparing for the polo match or whether he was avoiding her, she had no idea. It was none of her business what Nero was doing with his time. If she had any sense at all, she wouldn't miss him.

But she did.

The night before the ponies were due to arrive from England Bella slept fitfully. When she did manage to doze off, the young woman in the portrait seemed to come alive. With a fist planted on her hip and her strong jaw jutting at a determined angle, it felt as if she was sizing Bella up.

At one point Bella shot up with a start and switched the lights on. The room was empty. Of course it was empty, but when the cockerel crowed she realised it was time to get up. Leaping out of bed, she pushed back the heavy curtain. Excitement flashed inside her at the sight of a dust cloud that could only herald the horseboxes arriving from England.

Nero was already out in the yard.

If there was one thing guaranteed to bring Nero out, it was horses.

Heedless of how she looked or what she was wearing, Bella tugged her old dungarees over her pyjamas, adding a baggy sweater for extra warmth. There was no time to scrape her hair back, though she did pause in the bathroom to run a toothbrush over her teeth before racing out of the room and pelting downstairs. Tearing through the kitchen, startling María and Concepcion along the way, she burst through the door just in time to jog alongside the lead vehicle until it slowed to a stop in the stable yard.

'Leave this to the drivers, Bella,' Nero said sharply as she began to reach for the locks.

She was elated at the sight of Nero and feeling purposeful at the thought of the horses so close at hand. And determined to have her own way.

'I said leave it,' Nero snapped.

Moving in front of her, he said, 'This is men's work.'

'Men's work?' Bella demanded. 'Would your grandmother have said that?'

Nero's face froze and in that split second Bella said firmly, 'Excuse me, please,' and moved past him.

Bella was certain his expression could put a layer of ice on the lake, but Misty was in the back of this transporter and no one was getting in her way.

'Why don't you go back to the house and let us handle this?' Nero suggested in a more persuasive tone. She looked at his hand covering hers. 'I'll let you know when Misty's settled.'

'I'd like to do that myself. I want to welcome my own horse and check her over. I won't be going back to the house until I've checked all the ponies over,' she assured him. Planting her fists on her hips, she stared at him and he stared at her, neither of them moving.

'Shall we get on with this?' Nero suggested dryly as the back of the trailer was unhitched.

'Together,' she insisted.

Nero's lips tugged a little as he stretched the ironic stare. 'Together,' he agreed finally.

Good. This might be Nero's *estancia*, but the ponies were her responsibility too. They'd had a long drive, and a transatlantic flight and—

And standing up to Nero excited her. Her heart was pounding. And, much as she loved her work, she couldn't put all this excitement down to the arrival of her favourite horse.

Nero took charge of the lead horse, a towering bay called Colonel, one of his favourites, Bella remembered, while she took happy charge of Misty. It was inevitable they walked to the stables together—or, more accurately, walked to the small paddock outside the clinic where the ponies would wait their turn to be checked over by the vet.

'They'll be here for a few days of observation,' Nero explained as Misty whickered and nuzzled Bella. 'We'll keep her close for a few days, allow her to get acclimatised, and then you can ride her whenever you want.'

Bella's jaw must have dropped. It was the first time anyone had ever stepped in and told her what she could or couldn't do with her ponies. 'When I judge it right, I'll ride her.'

'With the vet's approval.'

'In consultation with the vet.' She had her hand balled into a fist, Bella realised, and it was resting on the top of the fence in a disturbing mirror pose of the woman in the painting in her room. And, just like Nero's grand-mother, she wasn't about to back down.

The sight of Bella, even in those wretched dungarees, stirred all sorts of unwelcome feelings inside him. Those feelings had only increased when she'd drawn battle lines between them. Why must Bella make his life so complicated? Why couldn't she just fall into line?

Like the girls who put him to sleep? The girls who had nothing to talk about? The girls who might as well have lived on another planet? Was that the type of person he would like to change Bella into?

Okay. He'd felt her passion in the barn. It was all or nothing for Bella. Sex without commitment would never be enough for her. Sex with commitment was something he had never contemplated. That didn't stop his happy contemplation of her naked body beneath the shapeless clothes as they led the horses towards the vet-erinary station. On the surface, Bella was ignoring him, but there was a current snapping between them as she whispered sweet nothings in her pony's ear. She was probably instructing Misty to obey no one but Bella—

And who could he blame for bringing Bella here?

No one but himself.

By the eve of the polo match all the horses had passed the vet's stringent tests, which was a relief. Bella had taken it upon herself to exercise Misty the moment the small mare was given the all-clear and now Nero was down at the corral with the other men, with his boot lodged on one of the wooden struts of the enclosing

fence as he watched some of the new yearlings being
put through their paces. He was aware of Bella coming
up on his right. He felt her presence the moment she left
the house and walked across the yard. He could feel her
quiet determination and confidence. Both were justified.
When it came to her job, Bella had no equal—other than
himself, and Ignacio, of course. When it came to caring
for the ponies, Bella's energy, intuition and love for them
was second to none—except, perhaps, his.

He could see her now without turning—her hair
would be scraped back beneath a net under the hard
hat she always wore for riding. He turned his head to
confirm he wasn't wrong—giving himself the excuse
that he didn't want any injuries on his conscience...

Of course she was wearing a hard hat. Perversely, he
wanted to see her with her red hair flowing free now.

'Nero.' She acknowledged him briskly without breaking step.

He dipped his head briefly in response. He wouldn't
see her again until she supervised the quick changes
from one pony to the next between the chukkas that
divided the game. Bella would be working with Ignacio,
which was a great honour for her. Ignacio traditionally
worked alone. But Bella was different, his elderly friend
had told him.

'She has the heart of a gaucho—'

He looked at Ignacio, standing by his side.

'She reminds me of your grandmother...'

Nero hummed and curbed his smile. Those few words
were probably the longest speech he'd ever heard from
Ignacio on any subject that didn't include a horse. They
were both staring at Bella, but he was remembering
the grandmother who had brought him up, and whose
portrait now hung in Bella's bedroom. In her youth,

Annalisa Caracas was said to possess the beauty of a pampered aristocrat. Nero knew she had the courage of a frontierswoman and rode like a man. Born to great wealth, Nero's father had considered a life of ease his natural right and had allowed the *estancia* to slip into ruin, forcing his own mother to come out of retirement and turn it round. It was lucky for him *and* the ranch that his grandmother had stepped in, and Annalisa Caracas was firmly placed on a pedestal in his mind.

Yes, Annalisa Caracas had been quite a woman.

He was jolted out of these thoughts by Ignacio nudging him. Bella had just mounted up and was turning her small mare towards the freedom of the pampas. He shook his head and huffed a laugh as the gauchos cheered when she set Misty at the fence instead of taking her through the gate. The small mare sailed over and then tossed her head, and in spirit so did Bella.

This was the first time in a long time, Nero realised, that he had stood with the other men to watch a woman ride.

CHAPTER TEN

THE polo match loomed ever closer and excitement was reaching fever pitch on the ranch. But it was more than excitement, Bella realised. It was as if they were preparing for the battle of the century. No piece of turf or rail had been left unchecked and her young charges were bursting with excitement. A sense of purpose had gripped everyone on the *estancia*—yet these were people whose world revolved around horses and polo, and who should surely take this *friendly* game in their stride?

Friendly game? Some hope, Bella mused. The team representing the neighbouring *estancia* were also world-class players, and although she didn't usually get worked up where testosterone-pumped males indulging in feats of macho lunacy were concerned, this was different. This was polo. But today even her great love for the game wasn't enough to stop her being anxious for Nero.

As the day wore on people arrived from far and wide. The match had brought the great and good of Argentina in helicopters, private jets and impressive cars, but there was also a large contingent of unsophisticated vehicles—trucks, horseboxes, battered Jeeps, cars with cracked suspension, rusting wheel arches and dubious paint jobs, along with a clutch of horse-drawn carts, as well as whole families riding in convoy on their ponies, trailing mules behind them, loaded with supplies. Polo meant fiesta on the pampas. It was both an excuse for a party as well as an all too rare get-together for far-flung families. All these people needed shade and water and food, as well as the other facilities associated with a small mobile city, and Bella and the rest of the staff had worked tirelessly to ensure that the event was a success. She was thrilled to think that everyone had come to see Nero Caracas, their national hero, lead his team. Nero represented everything that was proud and fine and wonderful about Argentina—her adopted country, Bella reflected as she stared out across the pampas. That was exactly how she felt about Nero's homeland—as if she belonged here.

And that was enough daydreaming when there was work to be done. The air of expectation gripping the crowd had made the ponies skittish—particularly Colonel, the pony on which Nero had decided to finish the match. In Bella's opinion, it would have been better to use Colonel in the first, or at least one of the earlier chukkas, rather than keeping the high-spirited horse until the end of the match, but Nero had overruled her saying his old faithful only needed time to calm down.

If only she could learn to calm down when it came to Nero, Bella reflected as he strode towards her down the pony lines. Surely, she should have got used to how he looked by now, but the sight of him still thrilled her—she still filled her eyes with him as she might have feasted them on a work of art. Nero was brutally beautiful, but he was more than that, she thought as her heart banged painfully in her chest. Oh, to hell with it—he was the sexiest man alive!

'Ready?' he said briefly.

'Ready,' Bella confirmed.

They had both checked the ponies numerous times. They were both professionals doing the job they did best, but that didn't cut off the electricity between them, or reduce her concern for Nero's safety in what was certain to be a fiercely competitive match.

And then the polo groupies arrived. Argentina was no different to the UK when it came to girls managing to look as if they had just stepped out of the fashion pages of some glossy magazine in this most workmanlike of settings. And here they were, complete with high heels and short flirty skirts, picking their way across a carpet of cobbles and horse manure. If she'd tried wearing shoes like that she'd have been up to her ankles in muck by now. She had to hand it to them, Bella thought as they clustered round Nero, the girls were groomed to the max. She couldn't blame them for their fascination. Polo was a savage game for rugged men, and horses as high-spirited could be found anywhere in the world. But as the girls fluttered round, and Nero, the king of the game, continued to ignore them and got on with his swift, practised preparations, she almost felt sorry for them. Almost, but not quite. Bella understood the tensions of the match and didn't expect Nero to pay her any attention, but the girls didn't understand that and thought all they had to do was look pretty and stick around long enough for Nero to turn and reward them with a smile…

He'd better not reward them with anything, Bella thought, feeling unusually moody as Nero turned to ask her for his stick. She passed it to him and, resting it over his shoulder, he cantered away without another word.

Taking her heart with him.

Don't be ridiculous, Bella told herself sternly. What was the point of giving her heart to Nero when he'd sooner have a bag of carrots for his ponies?

There was a tense air of expectation around the field of play. Everyone was geared up for action at the highest possible level and the game promised to be riskier than Bella had imagined. It soon became clear that, as she had suspected, this was no civilised knock-about between old friends, but a long-standing grudge match with no quarter offered by either side. There was battle fever between the players and, though Bella expected to feel on edge, she had not imagined longing for the match to finish so she could be sure Nero was safe.

Just let them all get through it in one piece, Bella thought as her gaze fixed on Nero. More the warrior than ever, with his tanned face grim beneath his helmet and his thick black hair curling beneath it, his muscles pumped and flexing and his strong hands on the reins, Nero looked invincible as he cantered round the field. That light grip was so deceptive. There was such power and certainty in it…and his powerful thighs, so subtly yet firmly controlling and directing his pony's movements.

She was jealous of a horse now?

The referee was speaking to each team. Silence fell other than the champing of bits. Anthems were played. The ball was positioned. Ponies jostled, and Nero hooked the first play clear.

The players thundered down the field with Nero taking an early lead. He was easily the most skilful rider. But even Nero wasn't invulnerable, and he couldn't evade all the opposing team's dirty tricks.

The other team's sole aim appeared to be to ride Nero off the field, and when two horses came cannoning towards him Bella screamed out a warning along with the rest of the crowd.

Nero would never risk his horse. Nero would rather risk himself—

A collective sigh rose from the crowd as Nero corkscrewed out of trouble, but it had been a narrow escape and, as the game continued, Bella grew increasingly anxious. The opposition wasn't interested in playing the game, they just wanted to create havoc with Nero in the centre of it. This wasn't about an elbow in the ribs or a well-placed knee in an attempt to unseat him, every action they took was designed to put Nero Caracas out of the game for good.

Yet Nero had never appeared stronger or more in control, Bella thought, taking comfort from his confidence as he leapt effortlessly from the back of one pony to the next between chukkas. This required split-second timing between groom and rider, with the groom having the next pony ready when the tired pony came cantering in, and no way was she going to let anyone have this responsibility—this was hers, and for once in his life Nero didn't have time to argue with her.

There was no basis for her sense of dread, Bella reasoned sensibly as the next chukka got underway. This was sport at the highest level and she couldn't expect it to be soft or easy. She should just relax and enjoy it. To see Nero at full stretch like this was a rare indulgence. She was watching out for risks around him, anticipating trouble even before it occurred. Nero shared this sixth sense and he used it to wheel and dodge his way out of trouble, while he controlled the field of play and kept his pony safe.

She was beginning to relax and enjoy the match, and shouted herself hoarse with the rest of the crowd when Nero whacked a ball halfway down the pitch and went charging after it. The other riders were in hot pursuit, but not fast enough to stop Nero smacking a goal between the posts. Rapturous applause greeted him as the teams changed ends, and within moments Nero had galloped in at the end of the chukka to change his shirt. Tugging it over his head, he displayed an obscene wealth of muscle to which Bella had to appear unmoved. And as if that wasn't bad enough, she now had to tell Nero something he wouldn't want to hear. 'I've substituted Colonel.'

'No—' Nero was scowling at the horse whose reins she was holding. 'Colonel doesn't have many matches left in him and I won't deny him this game.'

'But he's in a lather, Nero.' She shot an anxious glance towards the big bay it was taking two men to hold.

'It's your job to calm him down.'

And while she was still absorbing this piece of arrant nonsense, Nero mounted up.

'Colonel has been waiting for this moment, haven't you, boy?' he crooned, and she had to grit her teeth as the pony became both instantly alert and instantly cooperative.

'You'll never tame him, Bella.'

Was Ignacio talking about Nero or the pony? she wondered. 'It's a fantastic match,' she said distractedly. Even with Ignacio at her side, she had to brush off her growing sense of unease.

'Don't look so worried,' Ignacio said, following her gaze onto the field. 'Nero and Colonel have a special bond.'

She hoped so.

'I just wish this game didn't have to be quite so violent,' she confessed, voicing her fears.

'When you have some of the best players in the world on the field, competition is only to be expected,' Ignacio told her with a shrug.

Yes, but this was more than competition, Bella thought. This was war.

She'd never had this much invested in a match before, Bella reasoned as she leaned on the fence to watch. Ignacio had remained with her as if he sensed she needed company. There was only one man Ignacio was interested in watching, and that was Nero. She realised Ignacio couldn't have cared more deeply for Nero if he had been his own son.

'We're ahead,' Ignacio cheered as Nero swung his polo mallet and fired off another goal. The applause was deafening, but this became the cue for the game to become even rougher, and the crowd groaned when one of the riders was unseated.

Bella stared anxiously onto the field and only relaxed when she could see that both pony and player were unharmed. Her gaze flew to Nero, whose expression was thunderous beneath his helmet. She guessed he was furious at the risks the opposing team were taking with their horses. He glanced towards her and patted Colonel's neck as if he wanted to reassure her that they were both okay. She had to admit Colonel had never looked more alert or more impatient to enter the fray again. And Colonel's rider had never looked so savage, or so brutally attractive. She found a smile, though her eyes must have betrayed her concern and, with a brief nod, Nero wheeled away.

They were well into the first play when the ball

changed direction suddenly and a tightly bunched group
of riders came thundering down the field towards Bella
and Ignacio. Everything happened so fast—Ignacio
grabbed her arm and threw her clear but, in doing so, he
lost his balance as well as valuable seconds, while tons
of horseflesh continued crashing towards them. Nero
rode straight into the melee to save them. People were
screaming as Bella went back to catch hold of Ignacio.
Shoving him to the ground beneath her, she protected
him with her body. For a moment it was all a terrible
confusion of flailing hooves and rearing horses, with the
additional obstacles of boots, feet, thighs, bridles and
polo mallets. How they survived it, Bella would never
know. Her first clear thought was seeing Ignacio safe
on the other side of the fence as Nero swept her from
the ground and threw them both clear of the mayhem.
'Thank God,' she gasped against his chest.

When she turned to look, everything was slowly returning to normal. Reins were being gathered up, boots
stuck back in stirrups and horses were being turned by
their riders to calm them and give each other space. It
was only then that Bella realised Colonel was still on
the ground. 'I told you not to ride him,' she cried out as
grief and shock exploded inside her.

Dumping her on her feet, Nero returned to his horse.
'Get away from him,' he snapped when Bella would have
joined them.

Ignoring Nero's instruction, she quickly checked
Colonel over. 'I think he's winded.'

'And you know this for sure?' Nero's voice was ice.
His eyes were unforgiving.

For some reason, Nero blamed her for this, Bella
realised. 'I'm using my professional judgement,' she
said as calmly as she could.

He flashed something at her in Spanish that sounded ugly. It didn't need a translation. She understood him perfectly.

'Get out of my way,' he snarled, moving to block her out.

'We should help Colonel up as soon as we can,' she said, glancing around to enlist the help of Ignacio and the other gauchos.

'Are *you* going to lift him?' Nero rapped without turning to look at them as he knelt at his horse's head. 'Where's the vet?'

'Coming—he's coming,' Ignacio soothed in their own language.

Bella looked round with relief as the vet came running up.

Ignacio grabbed her arm. 'I want to thank you, Bella, for what you did—'

'Thank you,' she replied, holding Ignacio's gaze. 'We helped each other. It could have been so much worse—' Though she doubted Nero would see it that way, Bella thought, staring at him, shoulders hunched and tense as he crouched over his horse.

The game had been suspended and uneasy murmurs swept the crowd while the vet made his examination. When he had finished, Nero drew him aside so they could talk in private.

Knowing no boundaries when it came to the animals under her care, Bella followed them. She waited until there was a pause in the conversation, and then she touched Nero's arm. 'This wasn't your fault, Nero.'

The look Nero gave her should have warned her to leave it, but she was too upset by the fact that Nero had risked Colonel by riding the horse into the collision to save her. 'Thank you.'

'For what?' Nero's fierce black eyes drilled deep into her confidence.

'For saving me.'

The aggressive stare narrowed. Did Nero regret his actions? Turning away, he resumed his conversation with the vet in rapid Spanish, leaving Bella on the sidelines until Ignacio offered to translate for her.

Thank goodness Colonel wasn't so badly injured he would have to be destroyed. For all their power and bulk, horses were such fragile animals, but iced bandages followed by a stint in the hydrotherapy unit would be enough on this occasion.

They all stood round as a team, supervised by the vet, arranged a sling to hoist Colonel onto the recovery vehicle. Nero stood apart from the rest as the transport drove slowly away. The space between them might as well have been a continent, Bella thought.

Once the field was clear the game would be restarted. It was good news for a crowd relieved to discover there had been no serious casualties. Applause followed Colonel in his transporter across the field, though Nero remained staring after it with an expression that suggested the sky had just fallen in. 'It will be his last match,' he said to no one in particular.

And Nero blames me for that, Bella realised.

CHAPTER ELEVEN

'THE game is about to restart, Nero,' Bella prompted gently.

Nero didn't turn until the transporter had disappeared and then he said, 'Where's my next horse?'

She flinched at the tone of his voice. There wasn't an ounce of compassion in it. Nero was angry with himself, but he blamed both of them for bringing Colonel's career to an abrupt close.

And she was also badly shaken, Bella realised as she offered to bring a fresh horse up. A near fatal accident had almost taken out Ignacio, an elderly man she considered her friend now. Waiting for the vet's verdict had left her in pieces. *And the children!* How must they be feeling? 'I'm sorry—you'll have to excuse me,' she said, waving to one of the grooms.

'Where the hell do you think you're going?' Nero rapped. 'Do you have any idea what just happened?'

'Yes, and I'm sorry, but the kids from the scheme have been watching all this and they will be just as shocked as we are.' Without waiting for Nero's reply, she left him and ran. The sooner the children were reassured, the sooner she could get back to work.

Every cloud had a silver lining, Bella thought as she returned to the pony lines. None of the kids had realised the dangers of polo, and those who had dismissed the sport as girlie had been transformed into fervent fans, insisting polo was every bit as dangerous as motor racing and a lot more exciting to watch. Strange how fate worked sometimes, she thought wryly. And now there was just Nero to deal with. Her smile faded as she started to run.

'So you've turned up at last,' he said as he checked the bridle on the grey.

'Didn't the groom look after you?' Bella shot a quick smile of reassurance at the hapless girl whose bad luck it was to have her good work double-checked by Nero.

'You're in charge, Bella,' Nero said sharply, springing into the saddle. 'You should be here to supervise the grooms. This is not what I expect of you in a top-class game.'

'What else could I do?' Her voice was raised to match Nero's.

Grooms turned to stare as Nero demanded harshly, 'What were you doing on the polo field in the first place? This isn't a walk in the park, Bella, as you should know. How could you, of all people, be so irresponsible? What kind of example do you think you're setting for those kids you care so much about?'

She realised Nero couldn't have seen what had happened. He didn't know that Ignacio had almost been trampled. From Nero's angle as he rode up to save her, he would only have seen Bella staggering back as the group of horses collided with the fence, and had formed his own opinion. She was hardly going to mention that she had pushed Ignacio clear. She would just have to take this unfair reprimand on the chin. And smile sweetly. Until Nero turned his back.

'I'm not interested in excuses,' he barked, clearing

a space around them as he turned his horse to keep the high-spirited animal's energy in play. 'You never go near the fence again—and that's an order. And from a purely common sense point of view,' he added in a scathing tone, 'if you see horses galloping towards you, you back away. You don't rush to meet them!'

The air of battle was on him. She understood that. After a lifetime in polo, Bella knew that what appeared to be a society sport was, as the children from the city had so correctly identified, dangerous and demanding, and the top-class athletes who played the game were as driven and as fiercely competitive as their ponies.

So she'd make allowances. But she wouldn't be a doormat. 'I can only apologise,' she said, wanting to cool things down before Nero galloped off again. 'I'll go now and make sure that your next pony is properly warmed up.' The words were compliant, but there was something in her voice that warned Nero to drop it. Having said her piece, she spun on her heel and strode away.

He had felt stirred up in the middle of a match before, but never like this. But then he had never knowingly risked a horse before. And, of all horses, it had to be his old faithful, Colonel. His anger followed Bella to the pony lines, where he watched her working with her usual efficiency as if nothing untoward had taken place. Even that infuriated him. She was like no woman he had ever known before. He had risked everything for her. Why?

Bella's reckless behaviour had forced his hand. If she wanted to risk her life that was up to her, but in future he'd keep his horses safe. He galloped grim-faced onto the field. Defeat wasn't an option. Blaming Bella for her reckless actions wasn't enough. He blamed the opposing team for riding their loyal ponies as if they owed them nothing, but, most of all, he blamed himself.

Raising his helmet in a salute to the crowd, Nero acknowledged the applause as he led his team on the winners' gallop round the field. Only loyalty to the fans and to his team-mates was keeping him back. He badly wanted to be in the equine clinic with Colonel. He was desperate to check that everything possible was being done for the horse—and that shock hadn't set in.

Bella was waiting as he cantered off the field. She looked as cool as ever, while he was in turmoil. Kicking the stirrups away, he threw his leg over his pony and sprang down, thrusting the reins into her hand in the same movement. 'Ice immediately,' he ordered.

'I know,' she soothed.

The grooms were already waiting, he noticed, with iced bandages to cool the pony's overheated muscles. It was a pity they couldn't cool his overheated mind at the same time.

'Nero, you must take a drink too,' Bella insisted, holding out a water bottle with the tempting bloom of ice still visible on its surface.

Ignoring her, he moved past her.

She chased after him and thrust it into his hands. 'Drink,' she insisted, glaring at him.

'Can't you take a hint?' he demanded roughly, but he drank the water all the same.

He could feel Bella's concern following him all the way to the clinic. He'd told her from the outset that life here was tough. She knew the game. She knew the risks—

But she had never seen him like this before. *Too bad.* There was no room on the *estancia* for passengers. His grandmother had taught him that at a very young age.

'Nero, wait!'

Bella was running after him?

She not only ran after him, she ran ahead of him and stopped in front of him. 'What the hell?' He raked his hair.

'You won't do Colonel any good if you blaze into his stable in this state of mind.' She stood unmoving, glaring at him. 'I won't let you go in there.'

'Oh, won't you?' he said roughly, reaching out to move her away.

She slapped his hands down. 'Don't you dare touch me,' she raged at him white-lipped. 'While I'm here, those ponies are my responsibility as much as yours and I won't let you visit the clinic while you're like this!'

'Are you questioning my judgement?' he roared.

'Right now?' she roared back at him. 'Yes, I am.'

He walked round her. Had he really expected the Ice Maiden to tremble and quake like a virgin?

'I know why you're angry, Nero,' she said, running to keep up with him.

'Oh, do you?' he said.

'Colonel was reaching the end of his playing days, and you think you hastened that...' And when he made a sound of contempt it only prompted her to add fiercely, 'You did no such thing, Nero. You rode into danger to save the situation.'

'I had no option,' he flashed. 'I did what anyone else would have done under the same circumstances.'

Bella very much doubted it.

'If you will excuse me, I have an injured horse to check up on.'

'Then I'm coming with you,' she insisted, chasing after him.

'You've done enough damage for one day,' Nero

rapped, barging through the gate without holding it open for her. 'May I suggest you go back to the pony lines and confine yourself to bathing legs? Just make sure you don't get kicked by the ponies when you do so. We don't need any more slip-ups today.'

She fell back, allowing Nero to stalk off. He was without doubt the most obnoxious, pig-headed, arrogant man she had ever met. There wasn't a soft bone in his body or a kind thought in his head. Nero cared for nothing but his horses. He was truly incapable of a single caring feeling for his fellow man.

Which should have made him correspondingly unattractive, but unfortunately it had no effect in that direction.

It just made him more of a challenge, Bella realised, pulling out her phone and calling ahead to give the clinic a storm warning. Nero, a challenge? Yes, and professionally she could handle him, but in every other way Nero was destined to torment some other woman with more experience than Bella would ever have.

Having reassured himself that all was well with Colonel and that the horse was resting quietly, Nero returned to the *estancia* to eat and freshen up. There was no sign of Bella. He glanced up from the dining table every time he heard a door open or close. María and Concepcion were unusually subdued, as if the drama on the pitch had affected them too. He still couldn't work out why, for the first time in his life, he'd risked a horse. He ended up with the only answer he found palatable—he would have done the same for anyone. Human life was worth any risk he could take. There was nothing remotely personal about it. The fact that Bella was involved was mere coincidence.

He was in the shower when Ignacio rushed to tell him that Colonel had developed potentially fatal colic. He ran straight from his shower to the stable, barely pausing to dry himself, pulling on his jeans as he ran.

Bella had taken over the vigil in Colonel's stable from Nero the moment he had left the yard. He didn't know she was there. She wanted no fuss. And she certainly didn't want another row with him. She had agreed with Ignacio that, for all their sakes, it was better if she did this discreetly. And so it was Bella who had called the vet and sent for Nero. There was nothing more she could do, Bella realised, leaving a bowed and shaking Colonel in the care of Ignacio and the vet. Walking swiftly from the yard to avoid a confrontation with Nero, she saw him running from the house. She doubted he would even have noticed her.

She called in on Misty and spent some time with her own pony. The yard was quiet and there was no way she could know what was going on. When she left Misty's stable, she leaned her face for a moment against the cool stone wall. It was so peaceful in the stable yard after the high octane drama on the polo field. Squeezing her eyes tightly shut, she knew it was ridiculous to feel this way. She had too much emotion invested in a man who didn't have the slightest interest in her beyond her knowledge of horses. When he'd sucked that dry Nero would be happy to let her go.

And these tears were for Colonel, Bella thought impatiently, dashing them away. Straightening up, she lifted her chin. She'd check on her human charges next. The kids knew nothing of what was happening to Colonel at the clinic, and Ignacio had asked her to keep it that way. 'Not everyone has our resilience, Bella,' her elderly friend had counselled her gently. 'We don't know these children like you and I know each other, and we can't risk undoing the work we've already done with them.'

She'd felt proud at that moment, and touched that a man she admired had included her in his summary. Events had thrown her together with Ignacio and in a short space of time they had become close friends. The gaucho's friendship warmed her now and gave her courage. And Ignacio was right about the children, Bella thought as she walked briskly towards their chalets. Normally, she wouldn't dream of keeping anyone in the dark and would have come straight out with it, but these kids had a lot on their plates already, and it was up to everyone on the *estancia* to introduce them to different types of hardship sensitively. A party had been arranged for them tonight and she didn't want to spoil that for them. Without knowing the outcome of Colonel's colic, she had to consider that a drama on the pitch was one thing, but a tragedy might ruin the children's adventure on Estancia Caracas almost before it had begun. She'd tell them when she had some firm news.

The children greeted her warmly and she left them in the best of moods with the young counsellors the authorities had chosen to accompany them. She had another cause in mind now. Leaning back against the smooth sweet-smelling wood of the chalet she had so recently visited with Nero, she stared down the road leading to the clinic wondering what was happening with the sick pony.

What gave her the right? Bella thought. She was hardly qualified to offer therapy to anyone. She hadn't felt like this for years—so defensive. Perhaps she should take her own advice and leave Nero to it. This was a deeply personal crisis for a cold, sardonic man to whom horses meant everything. She really shouldn't intrude.

Nero had made it clear that he didn't welcome her interference.

It wasn't like her to give up either, Bella thought as she walked back to the house in the darkest of moods. Nero's feelings were standing in her way, and she was still fighting with herself when she pushed open the door of the hacienda. She'd have an early night. Things would look better in the morning. Whatever was going to happen with Colonel would happen, with or without her intervention.

She took a bath and went to bed, burying her head under the pillows, refusing to think about anything. At least that was the theory, but she was restless and sleep eluded her. She shot up with a start and glanced at her watch. 3:00 a.m. Whatever was going to happen to Colonel would have happened by now. She just had to know what that was. Nero would have been in bed hours ago.

Now the decision was made, she was filled with a sense of urgency. Not even waiting to tie her hair back, she tugged on a pair of jeans and a warm sweater and ran through the house, pulling on her boots at the door.

The clinic was unlocked and she took the narrow corridor with its faint smell of disinfectant and wet animals leading to the yard. Colonel's stable was easy to find. It was the only one with a dim light burning inside and the half-door left open. 'Hello, Colonel.' Bright eyes and pricked ears told her all she wanted to know. Colonel had recovered. And then something else stirred in the stable. She peered in cautiously. Nero was asleep on the hay, sprawled out with two dogs and the stable cat curled up alongside him. Her heart stirred. She pulled away as quietly as she could, not wanting to disturb him. Pressing her back against the door, she closed her eyes tightly. A man with so much love to give couldn't be all bad, could he?

She just didn't know when to give up, Bella thought as she walked back to the house. But why should she give up? A girl could dream, couldn't she? she mused, climbing the stairs. Nero was a product of his environment as much as she was of hers. So what if he was cranky? She was cranky herself. Add defensive, mistrustful, wary and aloof—oh, yes. She was a barrel of laughs.

First thing in the morning, she tacked Misty up and walked her round to the clinic yard, just to see, Bella told herself. There was no sign of Nero, and the veterinary nurse told her that Colonel had been released into the small paddock attached to the clinic where they could keep an eye on him. Colonel's leg was still strapped but the colic had passed, and the vet thought it best to keep him moving.

Thanking the nurse, she kept Misty on a loose rein and walked her as far as the boundary fence to stare out across the pampas. During her stay Bella had grown accustomed to its wild splendour, but today it looked so empty and not enticing at all. Take the romance out of it, and it was just mile upon mile of flat, open countryside, ringed with white-capped mountains showing faintly purple in the distance.

She turned at the sound of a horse's hooves. If there was one thing she should be accustomed to by now it was the sight of Nero on horseback. So why was her pulse going crazy? He'd been monstrous to her yesterday!

He had slept with his sick horse, she remembered, and was wearing the red bandana of a gaucho tied around his forehead, which was a very sexy look indeed with all that thick black hair tumbling over it.

'Where are you going?' he demanded, reining to a halt. 'Or are you just coming back?' His dark glance ran over her breeches which, clean of dust and mud, gave him the answer. Resting his fists on the pommel of his saddle, Nero raised an imperious brow. 'So where are you going?'

'Good morning to you too,' she said, turning Misty.

'Wait—'

The small mare recognised the note of command in Nero's voice even if Bella was determined to ignore it and Misty stopped dead, waiting for her next instruction. Not wanting to confuse her, Bella turned a cool glance on Nero's face. 'Yes?' she said.

'You need to be careful of the *yarara* if you're thinking of riding out,' he said in a voice devoid of emotion.

'The *yarara*?' Bella frowned, thinking only of the safety of her pony now.

'Poisonous snakes. It's the season for them,' he said before turning away.

'Wait,' she called after him.

Nero turned his horse. 'They won't bite unless you frighten them, but they will spook the horses.'

'Thanks for the warning.'

'Don't mention it,' he said. 'Just be sure you don't linger by any low-lying shrubs, or go rooting under rocks.'

'Is that it?'

'Should there be more?'

They confronted each other as if they were squaring up for a fight. Bella broke the silence first. 'If you've got something to say to me, Nero, just spit it out. It won't take me long to pack.'

'Pack?' he demanded with an angry gesture. 'Your work isn't finished here.'

Before she had a chance to react to that, Nero ground his jaw and finally admitted, 'I was wrong yesterday.' He raised a brow as if daring her to disagree, while she waited for a chorus of angels singing *Hallelujah!* 'I shouldn't have shouted at you,' he said, 'especially after Ignacio told me what you had done. That was very brave of you, Bella.'

'I don't want your praise!'

'Well, you shall have it.'

'I'll be sure to keep away from the *yararas*,' she said, turning Misty abruptly.

'Bella—'

She ignored him and the moment they were through the gate she urged Misty into a gallop. Nero caught up with her easily. 'You know emotions are heightened on the polo field.'

'I also know that's no excuse,' she called back. 'Your rudeness to me—'

'My rudeness?' Nero refused to take offence as he cantered easily alongside.

'You shouted at me!'

'And you shouted back.'

She rode without speaking, but all she could think about was Nero sleeping in the stable with his motley crew of animals and his sick horse.

'You came to find me in the stable,' he said, riding with all the nonchalance of a gaucho born in the saddle, 'so I can't have been so bad.'

'I was worried about your horse.'

'And me, just a little bit?'

'Not at all.' And, with a shout of encouragement, she gave Misty her head.

'But you will agree that it's good news about Colonel?' Nero caught up with her again and rode alongside as if they were trotting sedately in Windsor Park rather than indulging in a flat-out gallop across the pampas.

'It is good news,' she said. 'The best.' And there was only so long she could hold the frown for. 'Did you get much sleep?' she asked, trying not to sound too interested.

'Not much,' Nero admitted, slowing his horse. 'You?'

'Some,' Bella admitted, walking Misty towards the welcome shade of some trees. 'I woke in the night and wanted to check up on him. I thought you'd be asleep in bed,' she confessed.

Reaching for his water bottle, Nero took a long, thirsty slug. 'Do you have water?' he said, holding the canister out to her.

She wasn't falling for that again. 'I do,' she said, patting her saddlebag.

'Hey,' Nero called after her as she nudged Misty forward to hide her glowing cheeks. 'You forgot to tie your hair back, Bella.'

She was already feeling for the hairband on her wrist when it occurred to her he was teasing.

'What are you frightened of?' Nero challenged as she tied it up again, bringing his horse level with Misty. 'Are you worried you might show a softer side?'

'I'm only worried about getting my hair tangled when I ride,' she said mildly. 'And you're hardly in a position to talk about a softer side.'

Nero acknowledged this with a shrug. 'But I'm not frightened,' he said.

And she was? Yes, she was, Bella acknowledged silently—of some things, some men, but most of all she was frightened of losing control—of letting go. She hid these thoughts behind a counter-attack. 'You're the Assassin, remember. What do you know about fear?'

'Only a fool doesn't know fear,' Nero countered, 'but I'm not afraid. There's a big difference, Bella.'

With those dark eyes searching hers, she was glad of her shirt buttoned to the neck and the severe no-nonsense cut of her riding breeches. No way could this encounter be mistaken for anything other than it was—a purely chance meeting of the world's top polo player riding out on his ranch with a visiting professional who would soon be returning home.

CHAPTER TWELVE

FULFILLING her role as a professional judge of horse-flesh, Bella turned her attention from Nero to his horse. He was riding a magnificent black stallion, far bigger than any of the polo ponies in his yard. She guessed this must be a descendant of the Spanish war horses Nero had told her about. His mount certainly looked pretty impressive with its fancy scarlet saddlecloth, silver bit and the silver headband to keep its thickly waving forelock back. Nero wore silver spurs, and when the horse danced impatiently as he turned it in circles to calm it she saw that his belt was decorated with silver coins, and the typical gaucho dagger Ignacio had told her was called a *facon* was firmly secured in the back. More interestingly, Nero hadn't shaved and looked more dangerous than he ever had.

'How about a race?' he challenged with a curving grin.

'You are joking. Misty barely reaches the withers of that fire-breathing monster.'

'Then I'll give you a head start,' he said.

'Don't patronise us, Caracas.'

Nero's answer to this was a tug of his lips and a Latin shrug. 'If you're not up to it—'

Bella barely needed to touch Misty with her heels. The mare got the message and bounded forward.

A contest? Bella thought with relish. She was up for that. Let the best horse win!

'Hey,' Nero shouted after her as he took up the chase. 'Your hair's come loose, Bella!'

Bella's hair would feel like skeins of silk beneath his hands and her kisses hot. The thought of challenging the Ice Maiden to a race had got his juices flowing, Nero realised, reining back to slow his stallion. It would be the easiest thing in the world to overtake her, but that would mean the end of the chase—and, as any hunter knew, the thrill of the chase was everything—something to be drawn out and appreciated, so that the final outcome might be relished all the more. And seeing Bella crouched low over her pony as she rode with absolute determination to win this contest made him think the final outcome mustn't be too long coming.

They rode like the wind with no boundaries in front of them other than the snow-capped mountains more than half a day's ride away. The thrill of the chase excited Bella and, as the wind blew her hair back from her face, she felt this was the first time she had felt completely free since landing in Argentina—maybe the first time she had ever felt so free. The thunder of hooves warned her that Nero was close behind, the challenge in his eyes that if he caught her she would pay the consequences. She wouldn't give up without a fight. Goaded into renewed effort, she crouched low over Misty's neck as they streaked like an arrow across the pampas, but it was only a matter of time before the renowned agility of her polo pony lost out to the brute strength of Nero's stallion. Feeling the hunter relentlessly closing the distance between them stopped the breath in her throat.

There was something so controlled about it—so confident. Hot, hectic panic overwhelmed her and blazed a trail down her spine that spread across her back like cracking glass. There was nowhere to run—nowhere to hide—just miles of flat plain ahead of them. She would need a half mile head start to get away from him, and any moment now Nero would gallop past them. The anticipation of that was infuriating, and terrifying, and thrilling.

But Nero didn't overtake her. He must be holding back, Bella realised. Misty was fast but the polo pony was a sprinter, while a long gallop like this was little more than an easy hack for Nero's stallion. He should have disappeared ahead of them in a cloud of dust by now. Beneath her, Misty was straining to gallop faster. Having the stallion so close behind had unleashed a primitive flight mechanism in the mare. Misty's flared nostrils and laid-back ears were as telling as the arousal flooding Bella when she realised Nero had no intention of riding past her; he was wearing her down, knowing she was as unlikely to put her horse at risk as he was. Nero understood her a little too well.

Feeling Misty starting to flag, she steered her towards a covert of some gum trees. It was still a victory, Bella reasoned, slapping Misty's neck in praise as they slowed down. They had still won the race, and she had decided the finish line.

She was shivering with excitement by the time she reined to a halt. At least she'd made a good choice in stopping here—not only was it cooler, but an underground stream had thrust its way through the soft, fertile earth so the horses could drink their fill. Kicking her feet free of the stirrups, Bella dropped to the ground. She heard the chink of a bridle close behind her and then heard Nero spring down to the ground close by. 'Well?' she demanded, swinging round, hands on hips. 'Are you going to congratulate me?'

'You have my respect,' Nero conceded in a husky tone. 'You have a good pony, Bella, and you have trained her well.'

'Well, thank you, kind sir,' she said dryly. 'Forgive me if I'm wrong, but something in your tone suggests you believe you could have overtaken me any time.'

'And you don't think that's the case?' Nero raised one sweeping ebony brow.

A rush of excitement thrilled though her. She loved this game, loved the opponent best of all.

'You surely don't think you could outrun me?' Nero mocked.

She countered this with an amused huff. 'I did outrun you.'

'And now you want me to grovel in defeat?' Nero suggested.

Her gaze dropped to his lips, adrenalin still raging through her. 'No. I want more than that.'

She thought she was safe taunting him? Nero's head only dropped minutely, as if he were thinking about this. The next thing she knew, she was in his arms.

The heat of the chase had made her crazy, Bella concluded as Nero's mouth crashed down on hers—crazy for Nero. A lifetime of wondering and longing, and ultimate disappointment and embarrassment, was all worth it for it to end like this in a fierce pampas kiss—not a vain old man's kiss, but a gaucho's kiss—a real man's kiss—a kiss that was certain and firm, and teasing, and exciting, and so much more than she had ever dreamed a kiss could be.

Fire met fire. They should have burned each other

out. Not a chance. Sharp black stubble scored soft, pale skin. Pain was pleasure. The hot, experienced South American and the cool, inexperienced Englishwoman. Surely, it should have been unmitigated disaster—it wasn't. It was fire and ice, heat and need, action and pressure, gripping, grasping, seizing, holding, punctuated by groans of ecstasy and growls of intent. And all the time the heat was mounting. Even the horses had moved away. Who'd have thought it? The Ice Maiden had finally melted and met her match.

No… No!… *No!* What was she thinking? Theirs was a professional relationship. She had to recover the situation somehow!

Which hardly seemed likely when her body was an out of control, wanton, craving force. And if she was any other woman, it might be possible to go right ahead with this and deal with the consequences later, in a cool and professional manner. But she would never recover her self-respect if she didn't get out fast. She didn't have the savvy, the nous, the tools…

'Please—' Pulling away, she combed her hair with her fingers into some semblance of order. 'Forgive me…' She added a light laugh that sounded as insincere as it was. 'I don't usually get carried away like this.' All this in a cut-glass accent as foreign to her as Nero's South American drawl. 'The excitement of the chase…' She glanced at Nero to judge his reaction, only to find she had missed the mark by a mile or so. His face was a mask of sardonic disbelief.

'You'd like to talk about the scheme now?' he suggested.

'Yes, yes, I would,' she exclaimed with relief, blanking the sarcasm in his voice.

There was time to see little more than a flash of

movement—amused eyes and a tug of Nero's lips—before she was in his arms again. 'I don't want to talk,' he murmured. To prove the point, he teased her with his tongue and with his teeth, brushing the swell of her bottom lip with kisses until she was struggling to breathe and arousal hit every erotic zone at once, leaving her whimpering with need, and longing for release. But he hadn't taken possession of her mouth yet and, when he did, plunging deep into her moist warmth in a blistering approximation of what he could be doing to her, she responded as he must have known she would, by arcing upwards, seeking contact in a frenzy of excitement.

And Nero's answer to this loss of self-control?

He pulled away, leaving her in a daze.

She had been dazzled by the master of control. It was this foreign land and their exotic surroundings, Bella reasoned, the unfamiliar trees rustling a very different tune, and the small, angry stream bursting through the ground on its way to the sea. She was lost in a terrifyingly wild open space on a scale she couldn't even begin to describe.

All this was her fault, Bella convinced herself, tying her hair back in a signal to them both that this mistake was well and truly over.

Who was she trying to kid? She certainly wasn't fooling Nero who, having had time to process the data, was now regarding her with barely controlled amusement. 'Don't tie your hair up on my account,' he said.

'Lady Godiva of the pampas?' Bella grimaced as she pretended to consider this. 'I don't think so, do you?'

'Depends on whether you think I want to see you naked.'

She flinched inwardly. 'Believe me, you really don't.'

Nero knocked some dried grass from his breeches. 'Concerned you might disappoint me?'

'Concerned?' She laughed it off. 'Why should I be? And, anyway, as you won't get the chance to find out...'

'You're supposing I want that chance.'

But he did, Bella thought as she went to find Misty. And, more worrying that that, so did she.

She drew a sharp breath as Nero caught hold of her arm. 'Why do you always pull back from the brink, Bella?'

'I don't.'

'Don't lie to me—I sensed the change in you while I was kissing you.'

Her hand was already at her mouth. 'The change in me?' she repeated, pretending surprise though the proof that she had been violently aroused was emblazoned on her lips.

'You know what I mean,' Nero insisted.

Brazening it out and holding his gaze, she snapped, 'Do I?'

'I've seen you on the dance floor, Bella, and I've seen you retreat into your shell. What I don't understand is why you don't just let go for once—take a risk, taste life,' Nero tempted, refusing to have his good mood squashed by Bella's sudden change of heart.

'And if I did?' She laughed. 'I only get it wrong.'

'Do you think you're the only one who makes mistakes, Bella?' Nero demanded.

She had just thrown the reins over Misty's head and was about to put her foot in the stirrup when Nero held her back. 'When I was a little boy, idiot was my middle name. I was always getting into trouble. I never did what I was told.'

'Am I supposed to be surprised?' Bella said wryly, leaning back against Misty's flank. 'From what I can see of your grandmother from her portrait and from what Ignacio told me about her, I'm guessing she soon sorted you out.'

Nero laughed. 'You could call it that. She warned me that if I was determined to run wild, I should have a real challenge.'

Bella stroked Misty's neck. 'How old were you?'

'I was about nine when my grandmother took me for this particular ride on the pampas. We were both riding crazy horses.'

'Do you breed any other type?' Bella laughed.

'We didn't take a lot of food.' Nero's eyes grew thoughtful. There was a self-deprecating curve to his lips, as if he couldn't believe how badly he'd been sucked in. 'You think you know everything when you're nine—you're immortal and invincible.' Refocusing, he went on. 'Grandmother told me she wouldn't be out long enough for us to need much in the way of food.'

'I bet she did,' Bella said, her eyes twinkling. 'And you weren't suspicious?'

'Why should I be?' Nero frowned. 'This is my grandmother we're talking about.'

'Exactly,' Bella said wryly.

And now Nero was laughing too. 'I should have known when she asked if I had plenty of water with me, but I was very trusting in those days.' His lips pressed down as he rasped his chin.

'I guess we were both destined to learn our lessons young,' Bella commented. 'So your grandmother abandoned you on the pampas?'

'Yes, she did,' Nero confirmed. 'We made camp. She made sure I had something to eat, and then, while

I was lying back relaxing, no doubt planning my next mischief, she sneaked off.'

'And you didn't hear her ride away?'

'My grandmother had learned the ways of the gaucho. She tied cloths over her horse's hooves and led him away. By the time I looked around and wondered where she'd gone she was probably back at the ranch.'

'How long did it take you to find your way home?'

'Two days.'

'And what did your grandmother say when you finally turned up?'

'We never spoke of it—she wasn't exactly noted for showing her feelings.'

Like Nero, Bella thought.

'But she had—shown her feelings, I mean,' he murmured as he thought about it. 'In her way.' He grinned. 'Anyway, after that, Ignacio started playing a larger part in my life, or perhaps I started listening. I knew now that I would need all the tricks Ignacio could teach me to make sure I was never caught out again—like knowing where to find food and water on the pampas. How to catch a runaway horse. How to understand women...'

'Ah, the hardest lesson of all.'

'And one I'm still brushing up on,' Nero admitted with an engaging grin.

'And were you still a bad boy after this period of study?'

'What do you think?'

'I think you channelled your energies in a different direction.'

Nero shrugged and grinned back. 'I couldn't possibly comment.'

'So Ignacio has played a really crucial role in your life.'

'Ignacio and my grandmother were my formative influences. Everything I am, I owe to them. And that's enough of me,' he said. 'I want to hear more about you. I want to know if you mean to live up to your Ice Maiden tag for the rest of your life, Bella.'

'Maybe.' Bella shrugged. 'It hasn't done me any harm so far.'

'Hasn't it?' Nero challenged. 'Why would you choose to be that way, Bella, when there's so much life to live?'

She thought about it for a moment, 'Because I feel safer.'

'Safer?' Nero demanded. 'What happened to make you feel unsafe?'

'It was nothing,' she insisted with a flippant gesture.

'Nothing? There must be something to make you so defensive.'

'It's just so stupid,' Bella exclaimed with frustration, not wanting to talk about it. 'And the more time goes by, the harder it is to get past it.'

'Try me,' Nero said.

'It's not that easy,' Bella said wryly, twisting with embarrassment.

'It's never easy to open up and share things you hide deep inside. And if you've held on to something for a long time you can't expect it to come pouring out. Everyone fears they'll be judged, Bella, or that they're making too much of what happened, but that can't be the case with you, because you're so strong in every other area of your life except this.'

'All right,' she blurted suddenly, as if he'd lanced a wound. 'If you must know, when I was a teenager one of my father's friends made a pass at me.'

'And you kept it quiet all these years?'

'No one likes to be made a fool of twice. I didn't think anyone would believe me.'

'Why not?'

She shrugged unhappily, forced to remember. 'He had status. I had none.'

'Status?' Nero demanded as if the word had burned his tongue.

'I was just a kid around the stables back then. I'd always thought of myself as one of the boys. I grew up with brothers, remember, and so all that girlie stuff passed me by. I wasn't sure how to dress or to put make-up on without feeling silly, so my confidence wasn't exactly sky-high to start with.'

'What you're telling me sounds more serious than make-up and clothes, or even an acute lack of self-confidence. This sounds more like a breach of trust with long-reaching consequences,' Nero argued firmly.

'Anyway,' Bella continued offhandedly, 'when he left me he spread a rumour around the polo club that I was frigid. People started laughing at me. I didn't know why at first, but when it finally dawned on me...'

Nero cursed viciously beneath his breath. 'Forget him. Forget all those people. They're not worth remembering, Bella.'

'How can I forget them when that's my world?'

'That's your workplace. Your world is something different. At least,' Nero added wryly, 'I hope it is. What happened wasn't your fault, Bella. You were young and naïve, but you got over it. You're a survivor and you're strong. You built something wonderful with the legacy your father left you. I think you can afford to give yourself some credit for that.'

'You make it all sound so romantic—so excusable,

but I must have led that man on for him to try in the first place.'

Nero interrupted her with a vicious curse. 'How did you lead him on?' he demanded. 'With your youth? With your innocence? The man who did this to you isn't worthy of being called a man. His behaviour is not excusable. And being strong isn't romantic, Bella, it's a necessity. Being strong is what life requires and demands of you. When you're pushed to the limit you grow stronger and, whether you know it or not, that is what has happened to you, so instead of letting the past drag you down, take a look at what you have learned from it, and how it has lifted you up.'

'I couldn't fight him,' she said, lost in the past now. 'He was so much stronger than I was…'

'You don't need to tell me any more.'

'In the end he gave up.'

'Not for want of trying,' Nero said angrily. Bella's bewildered gaze had shocked him and the realisation of what she had been hiding all these years cut him like a knife. 'You must have been terrified.'

'Terrified? Yes,' she said faintly as she thought back. 'When he started laughing at me and calling me frigid and ugly, I was at my lowest point—beaten. But later, when I got over the shock of what had happened, I felt angry. When people joined in with his mocking comments—laughing about me and my father—it changed me for good, Nero. It turned me into a fighter. It made me determined that no man or woman would ever control me. And when my father's business failed I went to work for him. I wanted to help him rebuild—not just the business, but his good name. I wanted to prove to the world that Jack Wheeler still counted for something.'

'The Wheeler name counts for a lot,' Nero cut in.

'And that's thanks to you, Bella. Whatever problems your father had in the past have been eclipsed by your work in his name.'

He took her in his arms, feeling instantly protective, along with a whole host of less worthy feelings towards the man who had assaulted her. Without a mother to advise her, or close female friends to coax her out of her defensive shell, she had battled this nightmare alone. No wonder she found it so hard to trust anyone. Bella was the most thoughtful person he knew and only her complete lack of vanity and self-absorption had allowed so much time to pass before she unburdened herself. He was touched and honoured that she had chosen him when she chose to do so.

'Nero?'

He stared down into her wounded eyes. 'I wish I'd known all this before, Bella.'

'Well, you know now,' she said with the same flippant gesture, still trying to make light of it.

Speaking gently, he captured her hand and held her close. 'I want you to promise that you're going listen to what I'm going to say to you, because you need to hear this.' He waited until she relaxed. 'While you were struggling to take control of your life, you imposed sterner rules on yourself than anyone else would have done. You've been unforgiving where Bella Wheeler is concerned and you need to ease up. Let the past go, Bella. Let the bad parts fall away. You've got too much to give to keep yourself imprisoned in this Ice Maiden cage.'

She was hugging herself, Bella realised, releasing her arms. 'How can I do that when it still hurts every time I remember?'

'It will hurt less now you've told someone,' Nero promised.

'But it hurts now.'

'These are old wounds, Bella, and you just poked them with a stick.'

She had never felt able to share the past with anyone, or to talk freely about herself before, yet Nero had made her do that, Bella realised. For all his savage masculinity, he possessed some deep curative power. He was using it now to calm Misty. The little mare was impatient to leave and was showing off in front of Nero's stallion with head tosses and jaunty prancing, but one quiet word from Nero and she was still.

Bella was so busy admiring Nero's horse-whispering technique, he surprised her. Instead of mounting up, he turned his back and, ripping his shirt free of his gaucho breeches, he loosened his belt and pulled the waistband of his breeches down revealing the most terrible scars.

'Oh, my God,' Bella exclaimed in shock. 'Who did that to you?' The cruel score of whip marks was livid red and unmistakable. This was calculated cruelty on a scale that made her own long-held internal wounds pale into insignificance.

'This is my father's work,' Nero said without emotion. Adjusting his clothing, he fastened his belt. 'I was eleven years old before the beatings stopped.'

Around the time his parents had been killed and Nero's grandmother had moved in to take care of him, Bella realised. No wonder Nero had pushed himself and the ranch to the limit. Nero was as driven as she was in his own way. 'Your grandmother must have been horrified to discover what had been happening to you in her absence.'

'It was something we never talked about.'

'But it must have hurt her terribly if she loved you—'

'Love?' Nero murmured, appearing distracted for a moment. 'I adored my grandmother, but love was something else we never discussed,' he admitted wryly.

That made her sad. The way Nero dismissed love was an ominous sign, Bella thought, even if it was understandable. As a child, he had been denied love by his violent, drunken father and, with a child's stoical acceptance of what couldn't be changed, had learned to live without love.

'Things happen,' he said with a shrug. 'I'm only showing you these scars to let you know they haven't changed me—my father hasn't won, and neither must you allow what happened to you to rule your life and hold you back.'

'You can't compare what happened to me with someone beating a child!'

'And, bad as that was, somewhere out there will be children beyond number who have suffered far worse. That is why we are launching our schemes, Bella. You may not have thought it through as I have and come to that conclusion, but that is why you and I are so driven, and why you must use the past as a stepping stone rather than a barrier.'

The past hadn't changed him, Bella realised as Nero turned away to check the girth on his horse, but it had formed the man he was. Would Nero ever settle down, or would he never be able to trust enough to take the risk of loving anyone?

It all made sense now, Bella thought as she calmed Misty—her chats with Ignacio and the gaucho's closed face whenever she'd tried to ask him about Nero's father.

Estancia Caracas was a closed community where everyone knew everything that was going on.

'Bella?'

Refocusing, she put her foot in the stirrup and swung lightly into the saddle. 'Nothing's easy, is it, Nero?'

His mouth curved into a grin. 'You want easy, you could always go back to England.'

She shot him a level stare. 'And leave a job half-done?'

'Follow me back to the *estancia*, Bella.'

'Until we reach the straight,' she agreed. Challenging glances met and held. They had learned a lot about each other in a very short time, Bella thought, which, if they were to work together successfully, was no bad thing. 'Well?' she pressed. 'What are you waiting for?'

'I'm giving you a head start,' Nero told her with an ironic look. 'It's only fair.'

'Fair?' She laughed. 'I'll give you fair. I'll have a cup of coffee waiting for you when you get back.'

'Do you seriously think you're going to arrive before me?' Nero vaulted onto his horse. '*Hasta la vista*, Bella. I'll be in the bath by the time you get back.'

He stayed just far ahead of her to know she was safe. There was no point exhausting the horses, and he had nothing to prove. Neither did Bella. She had more than proved herself, Nero thought wryly. Everything he had sensed about Bella was true—except that her hunger for fulfilment went even deeper than he had thought. That was one problem he could solve. Her hair had felt like heaven beneath his hands—and her body, neatly packaged in practical yet severe riding clothes, had given him a provocative hint of the softly yielding flesh beneath.

She had stopped him because of lack of confidence,

he knew that now. Confidence could make a person, just as the lack of it could break you, he mused, easing the pace when he heard her pony falling back.

He liked her all the more for her unflinching acceptance of his scars. But Bella was as stubborn as the grandmother who had raised him. Like his grandmother, Bella would never admit to any inner weakness, believing it made her seem less in control. Unfortunately for Bella, he'd grown up with a woman like that. He knew what was going on.

He slowed the stallion to a brisk trot as they approached the yard. He didn't want to hurt Bella, but nothing had changed. He still wanted her.

CHAPTER THIRTEEN

SHE blamed it on the tango. Her neatly ordered life had always made sense before, but the tango made her confront her passions and accept that she was human. And it did all that—with a little help from Ignacio—in the first thirty-two bars. She wasn't exactly a new person by that stage, but she had certainly loosened up, and by the end of the dance Ignacio had managed to prove to her that as much as control was necessary to succeed, so was passion.

As in tango, so in life? One thing was certain, she couldn't go on the way she had been, marking time.

A number of parties had been arranged for the days following the polo match, and so she didn't lose face completely, Ignacio had agreed to tutor her in private dance lessons. The barn had a number of uses, Bella had discovered, and not all of them contained the dangers inherent in meeting Nero alone there. Ignacio came equipped with an ancient portable machine to play their music and proceeded to train her with the same mixture of firmness and patience with which he schooled the polo ponies. She'd never be an expert, she accepted, but she was a lot better than she had been by the time Ignacio had finished with her.

'Don't be frightened to let yourself go, Bella,' Ignacio

advised. 'And then the contrast when you draw yourself back will be sharper. You'll have people trembling on the edge of their seats,' he assured her when she laughed at her pathetic attempt. 'Bravo!' he exclaimed with gusto when she got it right.

Would Nero tremble on the edge of his seat? Somehow, Bella doubted it.

Nero felt her arrive at the party and his gaze followed her across the room. She looked incredible. The transformation from Ice Maiden to Tango Queen was complete, and was all the more impressive because of the contrast it drew between cool Bella and too-hot-to-handle Bella.

Too hot for any other man to handle, Nero determined, making his move. He bridled when he noticed the hungry stares of all the men present following her across the room. 'Bella.' He ground his jaw as one of the good-looking young stable lads got there first and led her onto the floor. He narrowed his eyes when he noticed Ignacio raise a glass to him at the far side of the room. Ruthless old rogue.

Nero grinned and then he laughed. It appeared Ignacio still had some lessons to teach him. And he'd obviously been busy with Bella too—boy, could she dance. They were queuing up to dance with her—boys who had hardly started shaving, some of them. And, of course, Bella being Bella, was only too happy to dance with all of them. She had so much joie de vivre waiting to burst out of her—something he'd only caught a glimpse of at the polo party in London. He raised a glass to Ignacio, who bowed his head in acknowledgement of the praise as Bella continued to dance with boys from the project, boys from the stable.

Men too.

He was at her side in moments.

She stared up at him. Her lips were full and red. Lipstick she never wore outlined them, enhanced them, made them gleam. 'Nero,' she murmured provocatively.

Her hair was severely drawn back, but he would forgive her that at a tango party, as the style was appropriate for the occasion. Her eyes were smoky and made even more lustrous by make-up. She looked and smelled fabulous—like a warm pot of passion just waiting for him to drown in. And the dress... What a dress. Low-necked and split to the thigh in shimmering silver, it was an exquisite example of the type of dress a professional tango dancer would wear.

María's daughter, he thought immediately. Carina was a famous tango dancer in Buenos Aires and about the same size as Bella. He had already noticed that María had made sure all the girls on Bella's scheme had the prettiest dresses to wear, and Bella's outfit was yet another example of his staff showering approval on her. He'd heard rumours that Ignacio had been teaching Bella to dance, and knew for a fact that Ignacio had found smart clothes for all the city boys to wear. But it was Bella, and only Bella, he was interested in now. There was a new confidence in her eyes, and the outfit, with those fine black stockings with the sexy seam up the back, had changed her, like an actress walking onto a stage she owned. If he waited for Bella to be without a partner, he'd be waiting all night.

And so he cut in. 'I'm claiming the winner's prize,' he told Nacho, owner of the neighbouring ranch, who just happened to be the most notorious playboy in Argentina and who was still stinging from losing the polo match to

Nero. Their black stares met in a fierce, no-holds-barred challenge.

'Would you like a partner who can show you how it's done?' Nero demanded when Bella hesitated.

'Get in line, Caracas,' she told him with a glint of humour in her seductive, smoky eyes.

'Nero doesn't wait for anything,' Nacho murmured, yielding as good manners dictated he must.

Nero stared with triumph into Bella's eyes. Remembering their last outing on the dance floor, he offered benevolently, 'I'll lead.'

'Into trouble?' she murmured.

Those lips!

Those lips were his. Firing one last stare at Nacho, he led her onto the floor.

It was like holding an electric current in his arms—dangerous, hot and impossible to contain or let go. 'Don't worry,' he soothed in a soft, mocking voice as she looked up at him, 'I'll be gentle with you.'

'And I with you,' she assured him as they waited for the music to begin.

He noticed how poised she was. She was a very different woman to the one who had taken the floor so awkwardly with him in Buenos Aires. Could this be the same woman who was almost, but not quite touching her flattened palm to his?

It was only Bella's hand, but he wanted it. He wanted her hand in his... He wanted all of her.

She evaded him as the music began and, with a provocative flash of her emerald eyes, she whipped out of his reach in a turn he wouldn't have imagined her to be capable of executing. He snatched her back again and held her close, staring down, imposing his will.

Raising a brow, she thrust him away.

His eyes assured her that he accepted the challenge and, when he drew her close this time, she had no option but to move with him. She fought him at first, and then she relaxed. They were attracting attention, he noticed. Or, rather, Bella was attracting interest. She was his perfect partner. The fact that they were dancing together, and quite so intensely, was drawing a lot of attention. He noticed Ignacio watching them from the shadows. The jigsaw didn't take much piecing together. Ignacio knew Nero had finally met his match and had enjoyed tutoring Bella so she could more than hold her own when they next met on the dance floor.

Hold her own? Bella was incredible. She set the air on fire, and everyone had gathered round to watch. Sensually and emotionally, she was transformed. It was like dancing with a different Bella—a confident woman who had found herself and knew what she wanted out of life—and she wanted more than polo. There were other gaps in Bella's education, gaps that only he could fill.

'Where are we going?' Bella demanded as Nero strode with her across the yard. She dug her heels in, refusing to go another step with him until he explained why he had taken her away from the party.

'I don't care to play out my private life in front of an audience.'

'I thought you didn't care what people thought.' She fought him, but his grip only tightened on her arm.

'I don't.' Nero stopped dead, his breathing heightened as he stared down at her. 'You look fabulous tonight, Bella.' And just when her eyes widened at the thought that he was paying her a compliment, he added, 'You could hardly think you were going to fade into the background in a dress like that?'

'Are you jealous, Nero?'

'Jealous?' Heat rose in his eyes.

'Do you regret dancing with me when there were so many more important women at the party?'

'What?' Nero looked genuinely bemused.

'Or don't you like my dress?'

'It certainly draws attention.'

A glint of humour was in his eyes and the glance he lavished on her now made the blood sizzle in her veins.

'And men were staring at me?' She struck a pose to stir him even more. As if she was on a mission to push Nero to his limits, she couldn't stop. Even his growled response and his grip on her arm had no effect. 'You were happy to call me the Ice Maiden along with everyone else, but now I show another side and you don't like it.'

'That's not true,' Nero said huskily, 'I like it a lot.'

'How much?' She shivered deliciously as Nero's thunderous expression changed to a challenging smile. He was playing with her, Bella realised as he released his grip on her arm. He was treating her like one of his ponies in the corral—drawing her to him, then casting her into the void without him so she craved nothing more than his attention. 'I'm going back to the party.'

'I don't think so.'

Balling her hands into fists, she thrust them against his chest, but from the waist down they were connected. There was so much passion between them now they could set the barn on fire. Had Nero planned to goad her all along? He did very little in life without a very good reason. Nero was the consummate seducer—of horses, women—everyone he met. Ice Maiden? Nero cared nothing for that tag. He had always known how to make her burn.

They should have made it to the house—to a bedroom—to a bed.

They'd made it halfway across the stable yard when Nero dragged her close and trapped her between his hard body and the barn door. With his hands planted flat on the door either side of her face, he nuzzled her ears, her lips, her cheeks, her neck, sending heat shooting through her veins to her core. Her breasts felt heavy and a pulse throbbed hungrily between her legs. And when she managed to focus at all it was only to see all sorts of wickedness in Nero's eyes.

She was drowning in arousal by the time Nero dipped his head to brush her bottom lip with his mouth. As his warmth and strength enveloped her, all it took was his lightest touch to fire her senses. The will to move—to leave him—the will to do anything remotely sensible had completely deserted her. She claimed one small victory, hearing him groan deep in his chest when he deepened the kiss and her tongue tangled with his. A lifetime of avoiding men had left her hungry, and now she found it ironic that the most masculine man she had ever met had freed something inside her, allowing her female powers to have their head.

Their kisses grew more heated, more urgent, until the barn door creaked behind them. Shouldering it open, Nero drew her inside. The silence was intense. It shielded them from the noise of the party, and when he dropped the great iron bar across the door she knew that no one could disturb them.

Kissing her, Nero backed her towards the sweet-smelling bed of hay. She kept hold of his shirt as she sank down, dragging him with her. This might be a dream that lasted one night, but she had no intention of waking yet. She softened as Nero pressed her to the ground. Each of his touches was a caress, and each glance a promise to keep her safe...

Unfastening the straps on her dancing shoes, he tossed them aside.

'I'm not wearing very much beneath my dress,' she explained haltingly, having a sudden fit of the same self-consciousness that had dogged her all her life.

'Excellent,' Nero approved, lowering the zip on her dress.

'Nero—' She flinched as he pushed her bra straps down.

'You're not frightened of me, are you?'

'You? No,' she answered. She was more frightened of the way she felt about him. 'I'm not frightened of anything.'

'Only a fool doesn't know fear,' Nero reminded her as his kisses moved to her shoulder and then the swell of her breast. And when she sighed in his arms, he took her bra off and tossed it away. 'If I ruled the world—'

'You'd be unbearable?' she suggested, rallying determinedly between gasps of pleasure.

'It would be a crime to construct lingerie out of reinforced canvas,' Nero advised her as he teased her nipple with the tip of his tongue. 'How did you fit that ugly contraption beneath this divine dress?'

'With the greatest difficulty,' Bella admitted.

'Are you a virgin?'

'What sort of question is that?' she demanded.

'It's a perfectly reasonable question. And if you are, now would be a good time to tell me. Come on, Bella, your answer can only be yes or no—'

'Or yes...and no,' she said, stalling.

Nero frowned as he shifted position. 'I think you'd better explain.'

When had she ever found it easy to discuss intimacy—or met a man who cared enough to ask? 'Of course I'm not a virgin. At my age?' she added with an awkward laugh.

Nero shrugged this answer off. 'Plenty of women your age are virgins—they haven't met the right man—they're flat-out not interested. It isn't a crime, Bella.'

Right. But she hadn't thought to hear Nero say it. She had always believed it was almost as taboo for a woman to admit to being a virgin at her age as it was to admitting she slept around.

'So what's your reason?' he prompted gently.

Surrender. That was Bella's reason. Loss of control. Putting her trust in someone else. She had never trusted anyone enough to be able to completely let go. But how to tell Nero that? 'People can control your life,' she murmured.

'Only if you let them,' Nero murmured between tender kisses. 'I would never do that. I have too much respect for you, Bella.'

She searched his eyes as Nero stroked her hair back. 'You have to let the past go,' he insisted gently. 'Learn from it, by all means, but move forward.'

'I have moved forward,' she said fiercely.

'Hey.' Nero was laughing softly as he brought her into his arms. 'No one's achieved more than you, tiger woman.'

'I had to…I had to defend my father.'

'Your hero?' Nero prompted, understanding.

'He was always my hero,' Bella admitted, eyes shining as she remembered all the wonderful times she had shared with a man who was flawed in the eyes of the world, but just about perfect where she was concerned. 'I had to stand my ground.'

'And fight?' Nero supplied. 'I know something about that,' he said wryly.

'I had to show all those people, Nero.'

'And you did,' he reassured her. 'Now it's time for you to think about Bella Wheeler for a change...'

And as he kissed her she thought that might, at long last, be possible—except there would always be that same thing holding her back—Bella's hidden flaw. 'I can't,' she said, pulling free from Nero's embrace.

'You can't?' Nero's ebony brows rose, though his eyes were as warm and as passionate as they had ever been.

'You asked me if I was a virgin,' she reminded him. 'And I don't know how to answer you because if I say I am, I'm not... What I mean is, I have and I haven't...'

'And when you did it was a bad experience—and that's what you remember?'

'Enough not to try it again,' Bella admitted, trying to be wry and funny at the same time, with the inevitable result that she ended up stumbling over the words. Her cheeks were glowing redder by the second. Closing her eyes, she tried again. 'What I'm trying to say and not making a very good job of is that I have...once, but I've never reached the ultimate conclusion that everyone else raves about.' She opened her eyes again. 'So you tell me, Nero. What does that make me?'

'A woman I want,' he murmured, drawing her into his arms. 'And if you haven't had an orgasm before, you're about to. So buckle your seat belt, Ms Wheeler—you're coming with me.'

And when she made some mild protest, Nero ignored her and removed her dress as if they had all the time in the world, and every inch he brought it down he replaced the whisper of silky fabric with his sensitive hands, or with his lips, or the nip of his teeth. Naked and exposed, her heart opened but, vulnerable though she was, she had gone too far now to turn back. The truth was, she didn't want to turn back.

Cradling her in his arms, Nero freed her hair and arranged it around her shoulders so that it framed her face. 'You're beautiful, Bella Wheeler,' he murmured.

She wasn't, but Nero made her feel so, and for the first time in her life she felt like a desirable woman. That feeling gave her strength and, unbuttoning his shirt, she pushed it from his shoulders, pausing only to admire the firm tanned flesh. At what moment had this hard, rugged face become hers to kiss? She brushed the curve of her smooth cheek against Nero's sharp black stubble and shivered with the promise of all the knowledge in his dark eyes that he would use to bring her pleasure.

Dipping his head, he took her lips again. 'No doubts?' he murmured, making her quiver as his hot breath touched her ear.

'None,' she said shakily. Torn between passion and fear of the past coming back to haunt her, she blocked out her past experiences and believed only in a very different future with the man she loved. Lacing her fingers through Nero's hair, she bound him to her.

Sensing her disquiet, Nero soothed her with a kiss, and when that kiss became heated he turned her, bringing her across his thighs so he could kiss his way up the back of her knees, her thighs and her buttocks until he reached the small of her back. As he cupped them, her buttocks responded with delight to each kiss and nip and stroke. She groaned with anticipation, forgetting everything but this, and even opened her legs a little to encourage him. Nero turned her so he could watch the pleasure building in her eyes as he stroked her into a frenzy of arousal. His hand found her heat and moved with an exquisite understanding of her need, but he drew it away, smiling faintly when he saw her disappointment. 'Not yet,' he cautioned.

'But soon,' she begged, writhing against him.

Nero suckled first on one breast and then the other. The heat of his mouth, the lash of his tongue and the rasp of his stubble all conspired to heighten sensation until she was completely lost in the moment. Laughing softly, Nero kissed the corner of her mouth until she turned to look at him, when he deepened the kiss and, drawing her into his arms, lay down with her on the hay.

'Now,' she begged him, easing down on the hay so that his kisses must find her belly and now the inside of her thighs. Shameless and determined, she thrust her hips towards him in a blatant invitation, crying out in triumph when Nero parted her legs with the wide spread of his powerful shoulders. Throwing her head back she gasped with approval.

But it still wasn't enough.

'I submit,' Nero murmured, when she moved over him and held him down.

'That's good,' she said, kissing his face, his neck, his shoulders, and then his chest.

'Don't stop now,' he teased her.

She had no intention of doing so, though she felt a jolt when she kissed the hard planes of his belly. He was so toned, so perfect. Nero was a playground of pleasure. And it was his turn to exclaim softly when she stroked his thighs, before cupping the swell of his erection beneath the straining fabric of his breeches. She measured and nursed it, and wondered if she could encompass it in one hand. There was only one way to find out…

'Feel free,' Nero murmured as she trailed one finger-tip down the cool steel zip.

'Shameless,' she mocked him softly as he locked his arms behind his head.

'You'd better believe it.'

Freeing the fastening at the top of his zip, she eased it down and he sprang free. Question answered: two hands. Lowering her head, she closed her mouth around him.

CHAPTER FOURTEEN

FOR a moment Nero was completely lost. He couldn't move, he couldn't think; the pleasure was far too intense. Bella had really surprised him. She was bolder than he had imagined, and instinctively sensual. She traced the acutely sensitive tip with her tongue, sucking and licking until he was forced to move—had to move if he wanted to please her.

Without losing the delicious contact of Bella's mouth on him, he kissed his way down her body until he reached the plump swell of her arousal. When she whimpered and threw herself back in the hay he stripped off the last of his clothes. Spreading her thighs wide, he found the heat at her core again and, laving it delicately with his tongue, he gradually increased the pressure. She was already moist and so swollen with arousal that when he parted her plump lips to claim the most intimate part of her, she widened her thighs and urged him on. When Bella's mouth and tongue began their work again, the exchange of pleasure between them was like nothing he had ever known.

Nero brought her to the brink so many times she wondered how he knew when to draw back. Was it second sight? Intuition? Whatever it was, she was pleased he possessed the skill. And, as for her fears of falling short as a woman—what fears? By the time Nero moved over her she couldn't have taken fright if she'd tried. She had never felt anything like this—had never thought herself capable of such intense sensations. Could it really get any better?

Nero brought her beneath him, positioning her as he teased her with just the tip of his pulsing erection. She loved the way he cushioned her buttocks with his hands. 'Oh, please,' she begged him. 'Don't make me wait this time.'

She heard herself add to this a brazen request in words that to her knowledge she had never spoken out loud before. Nero didn't seem shocked. He stared into her eyes and kissed her as he eased inside her, filling her completely. 'Yes, oh, yes,' she cried as he stretched her beyond what seemed possible. He waited until she relaxed before he moved again, and when he did she whimpered with surprise that such pleasure was possible as he thrust deeply before slowly withdrawing again.

'No,' she cried out, ordering him back immediately.

Nero laughed softly as her fingers bit into his shoulders and her teeth closed on his skin. She was soon gasping for breath as he started moving to a steady and dependable rhythm, taking her higher and closer to the promised goal with each firm stroke. Could it be possible to hover so near the edge and still feel safe? The tango might have brought her here, but this was the best dance on earth. She was rocking on a plateau of pleasure with a great dam waiting to burst behind her eyes and in her mind.

'Look at me, Bella,' Nero commanded.

As he claimed her attention she obeyed, and with one final thrust he gave her what she had waited a lifetime to achieve. Briefly, it took her out. Shooting stars invaded her head as pleasure exploded inside her. Sensation ruled and she embraced it hungrily, screaming out her release as the violent spasms gripped her, and they went on and on until she was completely spent and left to float gently on a tide of lazy waves.

'More?' Nero suggested dryly.

'Why are you smiling?' Bella demanded groggily, barely able to summon up the strength to speak.

'Once is never enough,' Nero murmured against her lips.

'You're so right,' she agreed on a contented breath. 'That was so good, I think you'd better do it all over again just so I can be sure I wasn't dreaming.'

Laughing softly, he brought her on top of him. 'It's your turn now. Ride me, take your pleasure. Use me as you will.'

She laughed into his eyes, feeling safe and strong— so safe she missed the flicker of something out of sync in Nero's eyes. She was still buzzing with how it felt to be liberated sexually—to be free and fulfilled. Nero had shown her that this was how it should be—and how it would be from now on. He was unique. Fate had brought them together. They shared so much—and not just this, she thought as she began to rock to a primal rhythm. They shared careers, and a whole raft of other interests... Nero was a friend she trusted, and now he was her lover. Could anything be more perfect?

Bella sucked in a sharp breath as Nero's hands began to control her movements. While one guided her hips, encouraging her, the other moved skilfully at pleasuring her. Her mouth opened in a gasp of surprise as Nero quickly brought her to the brink again. Lost to all rational thought, she allowed him to finish what he had so expertly begun and in the final moment before she took the plunge into pleasure she screamed out his name, and might even have whispered that she loved him.

Holding her safe in his arms, Nero stroked her hair until she fell into a contented sleep, while he stared unseeing into the shadows at the far end of the barn.

Bella slept soundly until a sharp ray of sunshine breached her closed eyelids. Stretching contentedly, she reached out a questing hand. The prickle of hay greeted her. It took her a moment to get her thoughts in order to process this. Party... Nero... Last night... Incredible.

And all these disjointed thoughts were bound by one certainty. She was in love. Nero was the man she loved. Thanks to him, she was transformed from Ice Maiden into something unimaginably different, Bella thought with a happy sigh, and last night Nero had put the seal on her love by proving that he felt the same. They had laughed and learned about each other and, trusting each other completely, had made the most spectacular love together.

So where was he?

She called his name, not really expecting a reply. Nero would be down at the stables with the horses. Considerately, he'd left her to sleep. He'd even brought a blanket from the house to cover her. Drawing it close, she sighed a second time. Did life get any better than this? She moved with remembered pleasure, but found it impossible to settle. The silence hung heavily all around her, making the barn feel incredibly empty, making her feel shut out.

So it was time to get up, she reasoned sensibly. She couldn't lie here all day with just a blanket covering her. Nero had folded her clothes. They were so neatly stacked there was something alarming about it. She couldn't put her finger on it exactly, but it could be interpreted as making order out of chaos. Last night had been chaotic and passionate—and amazing. Did Nero think so too? Or was he trying to make sense of the passion that had consumed them both?

And now she was overreacting as usual, Bella reassured herself. The Ice Maiden with her frozen shell and vivid inner life—she could put all that behind her now. Last night had changed everything—and she refused to think anything bad. Sitting up, she dragged the blanket round her and smiled like a contented kitten. She ached all over—in the most pleasant way. The impossible had happened. She had something going on with Nero, something deep and special. She felt like a real woman for the first time in her life, well loved and completely fulfilled. The Ice Maiden had gone for ever. Bella Wheeler had a new life now. Hurrying to get dressed, she threw on her clothes, brushed off the hay and didn't even bother to tie back her hair. What was the point when she'd leap straight in the shower when she got back to the house? And, anyway, well-loved women didn't bother with scraping their hair back. Flinging open the barn door in this new mood of abandon, she closed it quickly and then opened it a crack. Nero had his back to her and he was discussing something with a couple of gauchos. One of them was holding Misty, saddled and ready for him to ride.

Well? That was part of the deal. She brushed off any lingering qualms.

Once Nero gets used to riding Misty, he will never be able to let the pony go.

Nero should ride Misty—she wanted him to ride her pony. He'd been far too considerate so far, never trespassing on her enjoyment of riding her favourite horse—always giving way while she had been staying on the *estancia*.

Stealing another look out of the door, Bella's heart picked up pace. Nero was so poised, so utterly in command. The dark blue top emphasised his tan, and he was freshly showered with his hair still damp. Clean breeches, highly polished boots, and muscular legs it seemed incredible to her now she had been kissing only hours before. The conversation in rapid Spanish was indecipherable but, judging by Nero's gestures, he was telling the gauchos to take Misty back to the stables and get the mare ready for *Inglaterra*—she could hardly mistake that.

To hell with what people thought of her. Quickly, she slung the high-heeled sandals over her wrist and left the barn barefoot in her tango dress to confront Nero.

The men had gone, taking Misty with them. Nero was standing alone with one hand on the back of his neck and his head bowed as if the woes of the world were on his shoulders.

Swallowing deep, she could feel her own life splintering in front of her eyes. There was no pretending she didn't know what was going on. They had grown too close for the smallest nuance in Nero's behaviour to escape her. Her time in Argentina was at an end. They had always known this was a temporary arrangement. The scheme for the children was a success—they all wanted to come back and had promised to recommend the project at Estancia Caracas to their friends, which was all Nero or Bella had wanted. The prince would be pleased too, Bella told herself numbly. She had fulfilled her duty. 'Nero... Good morning,' she said lightly.

'Bella.' He turned, but the light in his eyes was swiftly dimmed.

He had made her strong, and now it was time for her to be strong for Nero—for both of them. 'So the time has come,' she said without emotion, angling her head to one side. Damn it, the smile wouldn't come. 'It's been—'

'Don't,' he said shortly.

'It's time for me to go, Nero,' she said as if she were encouraging him. She turned then and walked towards the house without a backwards glance. She had always known, deep down, Nero wasn't going to ask her to stay. Nero Caracas was a free spirit whose life had taught him that he could only be happy on his own. He had given her all that he could.

And that was a lot, Bella reflected as the shadow of the hacienda fell over her. Nero had made her believe in herself and in her inner strength, and in the beauty that came from a woman who was happy in her own body, and he had cemented that belief by making love to her. Nero Caracas, the Assassin, polo hero, national icon, the world's most eligible bachelor and most beddable man, the heartbreaker of Argentina. Why was she surprised that it hadn't worked out? She was a professional career woman, Bella told herself firmly, ignoring the tears battering the back of her eyes. Tilting her chin at a determined angle, she told herself firmly that polo was her life, not polo players—whoever they were, they were incidental—*which wasn't enough to stop her heart feeling as if someone had smashed it into tiny pieces with a polo mallet.*

She just needed a minute to settle her thoughts and then she'd get on with the rest of the day. The rest of the day? What about the rest of her life?

* * *

Nero spent the rest of the morning arranging transport to England for Bella and her horse. They'd use his private jet, of course, and with one of his own vets in attendance. He couldn't do more for Bella. He could never do enough for her.

And thoughts like those were where it all started to go wrong. He could see the future in Bella's eyes, while his was firmly lodged in his head. It was the same plan he'd had all along—be the best, make his grandmother and Ignacio proud—there was no room in his life for anything but the ranch and polo.

Nero's eyes softened briefly, and then grew resolute again when he remembered the hearts and flowers in Bella's eyes and the cold, clear thoughts in his. Rather than soften towards him, she would have done better to remain the Ice Maiden, for his heart was still the same piece of stone. He'd seen what families could do to each other—and knew he didn't want that. He wouldn't inflict that on any woman. What? And break her like a horse? Would he strip away Bella's successful career and dim that flare of emerald fire in her stare? What gave him the right to do these things when she had done everything he and the prince had expected of her and more? Could he take her pony? No.

Could he love her?

The only thing he knew about love was that it was corrosive and destroyed everything in its path. He refused to even think about it. He and Bella had enjoyed a great short-term professional relationship and that was it.

He should never have seduced her. He should never have enjoyed her. He would never stop thinking about her. His only option was to send her away before he wrecked everything for her. She must go back to

England, where she could continue her valuable work and pick up her successful career. Work was something he understood. Work meant building, as he had rebuilt the ranch. Love destroyed. These were some lessons a boy growing up never forgot. He wanted Bella, but what could he offer that wouldn't take her from the life she had built for herself half a world away?

Nothing more needed to be said, Bella reflected, which was both strange and sad. She had to go and Nero had to stay. She had started her packing straight after her shower. By the time she went downstairs Nero was in the kitchen drinking coffee as if it were any other day. It was every other day, but it was radically, horribly changed by the unbearable tension between them. She felt fresh and clean, neatly ordered and ready for work—with a yawning hole in her chest where her heart used to be.

'Thank you, María,' she said with a warm smile when Nero's housekeeper passed her a steamy cup of freshly brewed coffee. She turned away fast. She couldn't bear to see that look in María's eyes. How did María know? Was everyone on the pampas psychic?

This definitely wasn't the usual relaxed morning in the kitchen, Bella registered, feeling the tension rise to unsustainable levels. Nero finished his coffee. Putting his newspaper down, he stood, reminding her of how small she'd felt in his arms, and how protected.

'When you've got a minute, we should discuss your travel arrangements,' he said.

'Of course,' she said briskly, 'but I want to talk to the children first. And Ignacio. I want them to hear I'm leaving from me.' She swung round, conscious of María standing close behind her as if hovering, waiting to give comfort. 'And of course I'd really appreciate a few minutes of your time, María—I'm going to miss you all so much.'

Instead of answering this, María enveloped Bella in a hug.

And now they both had tears in their eyes.

'I'll be at the stables,' Nero said as he wheeled away.

As the jet soared into the sky Bella stared out of the window, feeling as though she was joined to Argentina by an umbilical cord and that cord was being stretched tighter and tighter until finally it snapped. There was just a solid floor of cloud beneath her now. She could have been anywhere—going anywhere.

Turning away from the window, her throat felt tight as she answered politely when the flight attendant asked her if she had everything she needed. Not nearly, Bella thought. The man quickly left her, as if he could sense that she was nursing some deep wound.

She stared unseeing at the dossier in front of her. These were the papers and photographs and the quotations from the children, which she had collected to show the prince. She could have sent most of it by e-mail, but wanted…needed, maybe, concrete evidence of her time in Argentina.

She'd miss the children, Bella thought, focusing on a group shot. She'd miss everyone. Ignacio, dressed for the occasion in full gaucho rig, positively exuding a sense of adventure and exoticism. The kids with their cheeky grins—long-time enemies, some of them, with their arms around each other, smiling for the camera—teams now, not gangs. María and Concepcion, their laughing faces so kind and smiling. And Nero. Nero towering over everyone in his polo rig, looking every bit the glamorous hero with the wind ruffling his thick black hair and his fist planted firmly on the fence beside him. No wonder control was so important to him. He'd seen where the lack of it had led, and what restoring it and going forward could achieve.

And she wasn't going to cry.

Who knew bottled up tears could hurt so much?

Picking up the champagne the flight attendant had poured for her, she raised a glass to absent friends.

CHAPTER FIFTEEN

LIFE went flat the moment Bella left Argentina. The atmosphere inside the *estancia* was instantly sombre, and the mood in the stable yard was scarcely any better.

'Everyone misses her,' Ignacio complained, stating the obvious.

'Do I need telling this?' Nero scowled at his old friend, who simply shrugged.

The last of the children in this year's scheme had just left, and the two of them had stayed behind to wave them off, but all the children had wanted to know was: Where was Bella? When was Bella coming back? Would she be here next year?

'Maybe,' was the best he could offer them, swiftly followed by, 'she's very busy.'

It had felt like a cop-out to him and he hadn't fooled anyone. To make things worse, Bella had left a jokey video for them all to watch. It had made the children laugh—and not just because of Bella's halting Spanish. He had stood at the back with his arms folded and his eyes narrowed as Ignacio ran the film—preparing to close a chapter and turn the page, but even he had smiled. No, it was more than that. He'd been drawn in. He'd grown wistful. He'd wanted things he couldn't have.

And now he felt wretched. The moment the lights had

come up he had acted as if this was just another day. But nothing would ever be the same again. Who could have predicted Bella would remember her first uncertain days on the *estancia* and could communicate the mistakes she'd made in such a hilarious and self-deprecating way in order to make the kids feel better?

Bella had given them all something to think about, Nero reflected, turning for the stables to saddle up his horse.

He stopped dead inside the stable yard. 'Ignacio. Is something wrong?' He had never seen his old friend dumbstruck before. Ignacio was known for being taciturn but nothing like this. Nero's heart raced with apprehension. 'Which horse is it?' he demanded, expecting the worst.

'You'd better see for yourself,' Ignacio told him, standing back.

'She left you a note,' one of the grooms told him, pressing a letter into his hand.

'Not now,' he said, in a rush to see whichever horse had succumbed to illness or injury. But then he halted. 'Who left me a note?'

'Bella,' the young lad said.

Ripping the envelope open, Nero scanned the contents rapidly: *She'll have a better chance with you—a better life.* Both the letter and the envelope drifted to the ground as he threw the stable door open. 'Misty...'

The sight of the little horse in his stable overwhelmed him. Sentiments he had never allowed himself to feel came flooding in. Bella had sacrificed part of her heart for him—and for the little horse she loved. 'How did this happen?' he asked Ignacio with a tight throat. 'How could the transporter leave my yard with the wrong horse?'

'Bella?' Ignacio said wryly. 'Bella insisted on over-seeing all the arrangements for Misty's transport per-sonally.'

'Of course she did...' A faint smile broke through Nero's frown. And she would have done so knowing that no one would argue with that.

'No. I can't do it.' Bella shook her head.

'But you must,' Bella's second in command in-sisted.

Agnes Dillon was an older no-nonsense woman who had worked for Bella's father as a young girl and now worked for Bella. 'The British team has asked for you by name. The prince has too. You're going to be supervising the royal stable yard, for goodness' sake, Bella—doesn't that mean anything to you?'

For the England-Argentina international? Yes, that meant something to her. All she could see in her head was Nero—the same man who had sent her a cryptic message saying: *Bella, what have you done?* But there was nothing to be done about it now. Staying longer than she had intended in Argentina meant she had come straight back home to a match. 'I suppose I could take the day off sick,' she mused out loud.

Agnes's wiry grey bun bobbed. 'You're never sick,' she pointed out, rejecting this idea.

'Then I'll take a holiday.'

'On the day of the most crucial match in the polo calendar?'

'Okay, I don't do either of those things,' Bella con-ceded while Agnes shoved her hands into the pockets of her faded raspberry-coloured cords and waited. 'I'll work in the background.'

'People expect to see you, Bella. Your place is on the

pony lines at an international. What's the matter with you?' Agnes demanded. 'You haven't been the same since you came home.'

No. She had been restless and anxious and angry that Nero hadn't sent her more news about Misty. She couldn't bring herself to phone him, but her call to Ignacio had confirmed that Misty was in the best of spirits and was being ridden every day in preparation for the season. And, yes, Nero would be riding her. Misty would be his first choice in all the matches. It would have been nice to hear this from Nero.

'Did something happen in Argentina, Bella?'

Bella looked long and hard into Agnes's eyes. 'No. Nothing,' she insisted fiercely, as though trying to convince herself.

Agnes shrugged in the way people did when they knew not to press.

'Okay, we've got work to do.' Bella shut her mind to everything else. 'I should get my horse ready. I'm planning to ride one of the newly trained horses in the last chukka in the women's match.'

Bella could feel Agnes's concern on her back as she walked away. If only the older woman knew! How would she handle seeing Nero again when she'd thought of him every waking moment since leaving Argentina?

She'd handle it because that was her job, Bella told her herself impatiently, mounting up. Her team was at the top of the tree when it came to horse management. Man management she'd leave to the specialists, Bella concluded, seeing a group of stick chicks wandering off to the bar. They had no interest in watching women play, but when the Argentinians arrived, like the answer to every woman's sex-starved dream, they'd be back.

* * *

The Argentinian contingent rolled into town like a conquering army—four-wheel drives with blacked-out windows, vans, trucks, flashy sports cars with exotic-sounding names, a couple of fire-fed motorbikes and what seemed like a constant parade of sleek new horse transporters. The glamour quotient in the prince's polo yard shot into the stratosphere as the polo guys and their skimpily clad groupies emerged to stroll nonchalantly about while the polo ponies with their massive entourage decanted exuberantly from their motorised stalls, tossing their heads as if to say, *Clear a path; we're the real stars of the show!*

With so much testosterone flying about, it was no wonder Bella had her work cut out keeping her young grooms in check. The brash new Argentinian horse transporters were like nothing they had ever seen before. The Argentinian horses breathed fire. And the men...

The less said about the men, the better, Bella thought, heart thundering as the swarthy marauders with their flashing eyes, deep tans and athletic frames took possession of every inch of space. Even Agnes had come over all coy and girlie.

Whereas she was attending solely to business, Bella reassured herself, checking each horse into the yard on her clipboard, ignoring the fact that her heart was beating a frantic *so-where-is-he?* tattoo. She was doing very well until a deep voice penetrated her thoughts.

Whirling around, she saw him at once. Nero must have been riding shotgun at the back of the parade, but now he had moved in to help bring a particularly fractious pony down one of the transporter ramps. Seeing him with his muscles pumped at full stretch kept her rooted to the spot for a moment. Nero was so much more than she remembered. He meant so much more to her than she had even realised.

But when a horse threatened to run amok, safety was paramount. With the carefully choreographed re-union between one professional and another that she had planned forgotten, Bella dropped her clipboard on the ground and ran to help.

Everyone else had backed away when she ran in. Corded muscles stood out on Nero's arms. He had looped the rope around his waist but, as the horse shrieked its disapproval and reared up again, something in Nero's stillness caught its attention. Rolling white eyes fixed on Nero's while flattened ears pricked up as Nero began crooning reassurances in his deep, husky voice. It was a sound that touched not only the horse, but Bella somewhere deep too. She loved this man. Love wasted, maybe, but she would always love him. She drank in Nero's resolute face and loved him all the more. Her heart and her eyes were full of him. Nothing in her life had ever come close to this feeling.

Finally, the horse was calm enough to lead away. Nero would allow no one but himself to take the risk of leading her and Bella hurried ahead of him to open the stable door. Her heart was stripped bare for Nero to trample on and only her professionalism allowed her to put her own feelings to one side and do what her train-ing, her life had taught her. It was cool and shadowy inside the stable. She had prepared everything for just this eventuality. There was always one horse, sometimes more than one, spooked by the journey and the new sur-roundings, and Bella's aim was to soothe the frightened animal with the fresh sweet scent of hay and clean, cool water. Nero was also the consummate professional and, having seen his troupe safely into the yard, he wouldn't allow himself to acknowledge the world outside until everyone was safe.

Slipping the harness off the horse, he handed it to her. They hadn't spoken a word to each other yet, but there was an incredible level of tension between them. It was like an electric current joining them. They didn't need to speak, Bella realised as they quietened the highly strung horse between them. In this area of their lives, at least, they would always be as one.

Satisfied that the horse was calm, they left quietly. Bella turned for one last look over the top of the stable door.

'All's well that ends well. Isn't that what you say in your country, Bella?'

Nero's muscular forearms were resting on the lower half of the door as he turned to look at her. Holding his luminous gaze, she sensed rather than saw the hard mouth soften. 'Hello, Nero.'

Warmth stole into his eyes. 'Hello, Bella…'

Their naked arms were almost touching, but while Nero might have stepped straight out of the pages of a fashion magazine and smelled divine, Bella was conscious that she smelled of horse and in her workmanlike outfit of faded top and muckers—the boots she wore around the stables—with hoof oil smeared across her stable breeches, she was hardly a contender for groupie of the year. She hadn't wanted to look as if she was trying too hard when Nero and the Argentinians arrived, but there were degrees, she realised now.

'How are you, Bella?'

How was she? She had planned to be calm and professional. 'I'm well… And you?' Such few words to express a whole world of feeling.

'I'm very well, thank you,' Nero replied formally.

Nero hadn't moved. He was just staring at her as if he wanted to imprint every fraction of her face on his mind. 'Bella, what you did—'

'I should go. I have all your documentation here,' she said, clinging to business. She handed him the pack she had prepared earlier. He didn't even look at it. 'I'll come down to the stables later when you've had time to settle in,' she said, turning to go. 'If you need anything at all before then, please don't hesitate to call me. You'll find my number in the folder, along with all the others I thought you might find useful.' She was looking into his eyes. She should have seen. She should have known.

The breath caught in her throat as Nero put his hands on her shoulders. 'No more talking, Bella.'

She weakened against him. When Nero kissed her it felt so good, so right. The scent of him, the touch, the taste, the strength. She felt protected all over again.

And knew how dangerous that could be. It was better, safer, to be alone.

'No,' Nero exclaimed fiercely when she tried to pull away. 'I won't let you go this time. I've missed you too much, Bella. I didn't know what I was losing, or what I stood to gain,' he added with a glint of the old humour.

She would not—could not—give way to the mael-strom of feelings boiling inside her. 'You thought I was teaching you something?' Nero murmured, staring deep into her eyes. 'But you taught me more, Bella. You made me realise how proud my grandmother would be of the ranch as it is now, how the team she founded has gone on and prospered.'

'How proud she would be of you,' Bella amended softly. 'Don't put yourself down, Nero.'

'Says the expert on such matters,' Nero observed

huskily, brushing her lips with his mouth. 'You showed me that history doesn't have to repeat itself, and that a life alone is a lonely life.'

'I've missed you,' she breathed, nuzzling into him.

'Of course you have,' Nero agreed with all the old confidence, dropping another kiss on her mouth. His eyes were dancing with laughter and the familiar crease was back in his cheek.

'You're impossible,' she said.

Nero shrugged. His mouth curved. 'I won't deny it, but I've missed you, Bella—more than you know.'

For the first time in his life he felt a little up in the air. He'd put his heart on the line and Bella had been called away. He knew she wasn't a woman to be ordered around or someone who would fit in to suit—not that he wanted that, but Bella was at the other extreme. This was a woman with her life totally mapped out.

Was there a place for him in that life? He had never thought to ask the question before. It was clear that Bella belonged here as much as he belonged in Argentina. Could two lovers half a world apart ever be together for longer than the polo season? With a vicious curse under his breath he watched her stride away. And then he shook his head a little ruefully. She was cool. He had to give her that. He admired her composure, just so long as the Ice Maiden didn't make a bid to come back.

'Hey, Ignacio,' he called. His face lit up at the sight of his closest ally and dearest friend.

'Can't stop,' Ignacio informed him in rapid Spanish. 'I'm going to see Bella. Can't be late; she's expecting me!'

He was jealous of Ignacio now? He felt shut out, Nero realised as Ignacio hurried off in the same direction

Bella had taken. At least he knew where he stood in the pecking order now. Try nowhere for size.

'Can I help you?'

He looked down into the concerned face of an older woman he remembered from previous visits. 'Agnes,' he said, remembering her name. They shook hands. 'It's good to see you again. Bella has made sure I have everything I need, thank you.' Except for the one thing he wanted, Nero thought as his glance strayed after Bella.

He was still grinding his jaw with frustration when he went to check on the ponies. He had wanted to say so much more to Bella, but she hadn't given him the chance. He had wanted to thank her for the movie she'd left for the kids and tell her how they had used it for each new intake—and that they would need a new film for next year. He had thought about their reunion constantly since she'd left, but he had pictured something very different—fireworks, not business. It was always duty first for Bella.

But now duty called him too. Work soothed him. The ponies always soothed him. And Bella would be back at his side as soon as she had finished whatever it was she had left him to do.

Bella wasn't back at his side, later that day or the next. Having made discreet enquiries, he learned she was evaluating the fitness of borderline match-ready ponies. Ignacio was his usual taciturn self and, in spite of Nero's subtle and not-so-subtle prompting, Ignacio refused to let anything slip about his own reunion with Bella. So had they talked about him at all? Or was work really all that mattered to Bella? And why was he feeling so indignant when it was the same for him? He had a week of non-stop training and preparation until the match ahead of him.

The day of the game matched his mood, with grim grey skies and rolling clouds of ink-lined pewter. He had only dozed on and off through another lonely night. How was Bella? Had she slept well? Selfishly, he hoped not. He hoped, like him, she hadn't slept properly all week.

Peering out of the window of his hotel, which was located on the fringes of the polo club, he had a good view of the pitch. Slippery, he determined, and the weather wasn't going to get better any time soon. He let the curtain fall back.

Drying off after an ice-cold shower, he switched on the news in time to catch the weather forecast. Thunder predicted later. Brilliant. Just what the horses didn't like. Bella would need all the help she could get to keep them calm. Sensing electricity in the air, they would be restless. It was one thing staying out of Bella's private life, but where work was involved her safety was his concern. And at work was the only time he'd seen her this week, at a joint team briefing. And each time when tension snapped between them she found some excuse to hurry away.

The time had come to change that for good.

Bella enjoyed her time with Ignacio, asking him questions about Nero's wild youth. Of course, she knew there were areas where she shouldn't trespass. Nero had told her about his parents—his father, in particular, and she wouldn't stretch the elderly gaucho's patience by delving into a past that he wouldn't care to remember, but he did give one reason why Nero had difficulty expressing his feelings. 'It's the gaucho's way,' Ignacio told her.

Ignacio had been a huge influence on Nero's life, stepping in and teaching him all his grandmother's tricks, as well as a few of his own. But there were other reasons for Nero's solitary path through life, his horrific childhood for one. When he should have known love and protection, Nero had faced cruelty and uncertainty. But if she could put her past behind her—

'Are all the ponies match-ready?'

She jumped guiltily at the sound of Nero's voice. 'All the ponies on this side of the yard have been passed by the vet.'

Without a word, Ignacio gathered up his grooming tackle and left them.

'What do *you* think, Bella?' Nero pressed.

'I think the weather conditions are treacherous and likely to get worse,' she said, holding Nero's fierce stare. 'I think the ponies are in great condition, but you need to take care. The ground will be slippery and your ponies don't like the wet, whereas our English ponies are used to damp conditions.' Her heart was pounding with concern and with longing.

'And your English ponies are unlike every other breed on the planet in that they're used to thunder, are they?' Nero demanded. With a sceptical huff, he flicked a look at the sky.

'We'll just have to hope the storm holds off.'

'Well, whatever happens, no more heroics from you. No more straying onto the pitch. For whatever reason,' Nero insisted, dipping his handsome head to stare her in the eyes. 'Do you understand me?'

'I thought we had that squared away.'

'We have, but I haven't forgotten.'

She let out a shaking breath as he strode away. Would things ever be relaxed and easy between them again?

Since his return it felt as if Nero had seized hold of her life and tossed it into the path of a hurricane.

Yes, and when he left she'd be in the doldrums again. Even if they hardly spoke now, she dreaded him leaving. She dreaded facing another endless span of unbearable longing. Resting her face against the warm, firm neck of the pony she'd been grooming, Bella vowed not to waste another second of her life thinking about Nero. Time was such a fragile, fleeting thing, and he would soon be going home to Argentina.

CHAPTER SIXTEEN

THE thunder held off, though Bella had been right about the ponies. The ground was wet and more than one pony had gone lame after skidding to a halt. The pony Nero was riding in this chukka had cast a shoe. 'Where is she?' he demanded when he rode in. 'Where's Bella?'

'She's with the grooms, warming up the ponies,' Agnes explained as he swung down from the saddle.

'She should be here.' He gazed up and down the pony lines, searching for her. 'It's her job to be here.' He pulled off his helmet as the horn sounded, announcing the end of the first half.

Meanwhile, Agnes was wringing her hands, which was most unlike her. 'What's the matter, Agnes?'

'We're short of horses, or I'd have another one brought up for you right away.'

'Don't worry; it's not your fault. These are unusual weather conditions. The match should have been cancelled.'

'Such an important match?' Agnes appeared horror-struck.

'Why not?' he said. 'It's only a game.' Words he thought he'd never hear himself say twice in one lifetime. He turned to see Bella leading Misty towards them. 'What are you doing?' he said suspiciously. 'I heard you'd run out of horses.'

'Not quite,' Bella said as she patted the pony's neck.

'You have to be joking. I'm not risking Misty. I brought her back to England where she belongs—with you. Have you seen the weather conditions? It's carnage out there.' And his emotions were all over the place. Bella was offering him her pony, a symbol of everything she cared about. 'I won't ride her,' he said decisively.

'She's equal to anything out there.'

'The brutality?'

'She'll keep you safe, Nero.'

There was so much in Bella's steady gaze, he seized her in front of everyone and brought her close. They stared into each other's eyes for a moment, for a lifetime, for eternity. 'Don't you ever stay away from me again,' he ground out.

'It's been a week,' she teased him.

'A week too long,' he argued, kissing her with hungry passion. He cursed impatiently as the horn sounded, calling him back onto the field.

'I'll be waiting for you,' she called after him, levelling that same steady stare on his face.

'I'll take care of her,' he promised, vaulting onto Misty's back. As he settled his helmet on his head he was suddenly aware that Bella and he were the focus of everyone's attention, from the grooms to Ignacio, and from the stick chicks to the prince, who had come to inspect his horses. 'I love you, Bella Wheeler,' he called out as everyone cheered. 'I've always loved you and I always will.' And he didn't care who heard.

'I love you too,' she said, her face as bright as the sun peeping through the clouds. 'Stay safe!'

Removing his helmet, he saluted her with a bow. He'd

won the only match he cared about. He hadn't a clue how Bella and he were going to make it work; he only knew they would.

They drank a toast to the victory of Nero's team. It was a massive victory, as the prince was the first to admit. He could hardly blame Bella for allowing the captain of the Argentinian team to ride her best pony, when it was the prince who had suggested that the best polo player in the world ought to be matched with Misty. He just hadn't factored the timing into his thinking, the prince admitted wryly. Just as he hadn't realised what a wonderful job Bella had done in Argentina, he added, thanking her for the portfolio of her stay she'd compiled for him. 'You must go back there,' the prince insisted. 'Agnes and my team can hold the fort for you here.'

'You're too kind, Sir,' Bella said, glancing at Nero.

The moment the prince's back was turned, Nero grabbed hold of her hand. 'You, me. Quiet time, now,' he insisted, leading Bella away. 'You can't refuse a royal command,' he reminded her, tongue in cheek, 'though I don't need the prince to prompt me.'

Bella curbed a smile. 'I've got something for you,' she said softly.

'And I've got something I want to tell you,' he said, drawing her to a halt in the grand, ornately plastered hallway of the Polo Club.

'Present first,' Bella insisted. Ignacio had told her that although Nero was the most generous of men, he frowned on his staff spending their hard-earned money on him. And, as he had no living relatives, Nero didn't exactly get a full Christmas sack. Bella intended to change that.

Nero looked suspicious. 'Is Ignacio in on this?'

'If he is I wouldn't tell you.'

'Will I like it?'

'Oh, I think so,' she said confidently.

He must be patient, Nero thought as Bella led him back across the polo ground towards the stables. What he had to say to her had waited long enough—it could wait a little longer. Bella touched him more than any woman ever had. Like now, when she was clutching her breast above her heart as she took him across the yard towards an emerald-green paddock that stretched down to the river. The paddock was home to a herd of spirited young colts, currently racing around, testing each other.

'The grey,' Bella said, pointing. 'That's Misty's first colt. He was born before I even met you, but he's two years old now, ready to start polo training.'

She stared up at him. 'He's a fine pony.' Nero's eyes narrowed as he watched the young horse go through his paces. 'A little wild, but courage and daring is what I always look for.' His gaze was drawn to Bella. 'You've done well,' he said, 'really well.'

'I named him Tango. For you.'

He inhaled sharply. 'For me?'

'It's my gift to you,' she explained, 'for your…hospitality in Argentina.'

He was incredulous. No one had ever given him anything of such great value before. He threw her a crooked smile. 'I'm glad you enjoyed yourself.'

'Oh, I did. And now at least you can breed some decent animals from those Criollas of yours,' she teased him, tilting her chin at the familiar challenging angle.

'Cheeky,' he warned, but he was laughing too. He wondered if he had ever been so happy in his life.

'Hopefully, a few years down the line your polo

ponies will be able to keep their feet when they come to England.' She turned serious. 'Tango has a great bloodline, Nero, and I think he'll be happy with those pretty mares of yours on the pampas.'

'Bella, I don't know what to say.'

'Don't say anything.'

'What can I give you in return?'

'I don't want anything in return—I never have.'

'May I give you my heart?' He stared down, realising that this was the single most important question he had ever asked in his life, and that Bella's answer would change both their lives for ever.

The solution was simple. The solution had been in front of them all the time, which was probably why they hadn't seen it and the prince had, Bella realised as she tried on the wedding dress in the thirty-third shop in at least the sixth country on the polo tour. But this one was perfect, which was just as well, since it was essential she found one before Nero came back to drag her out of the shop. Patience was not one of his virtues. A special licence and the two of them was all that was required—Bella had different ideas. She wanted photographs for their children to remember. So here she was in the most exclusive wedding store in Rome.

As the murmuring attendants fussed around her, Bella allowed herself a moment of quiet reflection. After their wedding, she would be back in Argentina with Nero in time for the new intake of children on the scheme and for the polo season there. They would then both travel back to the northern hemisphere in time to manage Bella's projects. But, more important than all of this, Nero insisted, was the life they built together. Remembering the portrait of his grandmother, Bella knew she would be following her heart to the pampas, just as Nero would be following his head when he came to England to play polo for the prince.

She was jolted out of these thoughts by Nero throwing the assistants into a panic by striding unannounced into a wedding boutique that suddenly seemed far too small to hold both Nero Caracas and the chosen wedding dress. Barring the entrance to her cubicle, the brave women held him at bay.

'Get me out of this,' Bella exclaimed, already tearing at the laces.

The women only just managed to remove the gown in time and hide it as Nero threw back the curtain.

'Don't test me, Bella.'

The women scattered, leaving them alone.

Bella levelled a stare on Nero's face as his fierce expression mellowed into a lazy gaze. 'Do you like it?' she asked, modelling the new underwear he'd bought her.

'It's a great improvement on industrial weight serge and heavy engineering.'

And she would never have bought such inconsequential scraps of lace for herself, or dreamed of wearing such things before she met Nero but, thanks to him, the damage of the past was nothing more than a reminder of how lucky they were to have found each other.

'We are in the city of lovers,' Nero murmured, running the knuckles of one hand very lightly down her cheek, 'so I shall test you later, to see if the new lingerie is having the required effect.'

'Excellent,' Bella agreed softly. 'The Ice Maiden is already melting in anticipation of your prolonged attention.' Catching hold of his hand, she kissed it whilst holding his gaze.

'You're my world, Bella,' Nero said, turning suddenly serious as he cupped her face between his hands. 'And after this tour we're going to stay home in Argentina and raise ponies together.'

'What?' And then she saw the laughter in his eyes.

'Did I say ponies?' Nero murmured.

'You know you did. Nero—stop,' she begged him as his kisses migrated from her mouth to her neck and from her neck to her breast. 'We're not alone.'

'When in Rome...' he murmured, clasping her to him.

'But the women in the shop...'

'Have seen it all before.'

'We can't.'

'No, you're right,' Nero agreed, leaving her weak and trembling as he removed his hand. 'We may need some time, so I'm going to make you wait until we get back to the hotel. All those years of work and no play have made Bella a very naughty girl indeed.'

'And you, of course, are absolutely innocent,' she commented wryly.

'No, *chica*,' Nero murmured against her mouth, 'I'm a very bad man indeed.'

All Bella could hear was the beating of her heart. 'Yes, yes...*Yes!*' she agreed in a heated whisper, 'Promise we can keep it that way...'

* * * * *

AUGUST 2011 HARDBACK TITLES

ROMANCE

Bride for Real	Lynne Graham
From Dirt to Diamonds	Julia James
The Thorn in His Side	Kim Lawrence
Fiancée for One Night	Trish Morey
The Untamed Argentinian	Susan Stephens
After the Greek Affair	Chantelle Shaw
The Highest Price to Pay	Maisey Yates
Under the Brazilian Sun	Catherine George
There's Something About a Rebel...	Anne Oliver
The Crown Affair	Lucy King
Australia's Maverick Millionaire	Margaret Way
Rescued by the Brooding Tycoon	Lucy Gordon
Not-So-Perfect Princess	Melissa McClone
The Heart of a Hero	Barbara Wallace
Swept Off Her Stilettos	Fiona Harper
Mr Right There All Along	Jackie Braun
The Tortured Rebel	Alison Roberts
Dating Dr Delicious	Laura Iding

HISTORICAL

Married to a Stranger	Louise Allen
A Dark and Brooding Gentleman	Margaret McPhee
Seducing Miss Lockwood	Helen Dickson
The Highlander's Return	Marguerite Kaye

MEDICAL™

The Doctor's Reason to Stay	Dianne Drake
Career Girl in the Country	Fiona Lowe
Wedding on the Baby Ward	Lucy Clark
Special Care Baby Miracle	Lucy Clark

0711 Gen Std LP

 MILLS BOON®

AUGUST 2011
LARGE PRINT TITLES

ROMANCE

Jess's Promise	Lynne Graham
Not For Sale	Sandra Marton
After Their Vows	Michelle Reid
A Spanish Awakening	Kim Lawrence
In the Australian Billionaire's Arms	Margaret Way
Abby and the Bachelor Cop	Marion Lennox
Misty and the Single Dad	Marion Lennox
Daycare Mum to Wife	Jennie Adams

HISTORICAL

Miss in a Man's World	Anne Ashley
Captain Corcoran's Hoyden Bride	Annie Burrows
His Counterfeit Condesa	Joanna Fulford
Rebellious Rake, Innocent Governess	Elizabeth Beacon

MEDICAL™

Cedar Bluff's Most Eligible Bachelor	Laura Iding
Doctor: Diamond in the Rough	Lucy Clark
Becoming Dr Bellini's Bride	Joanna Neil
Midwife, Mother...Italian's Wife	Fiona McArthur
St Piran's: Daredevil, Doctor...Dad!	Anne Fraser
Single Dad's Triple Trouble	Fiona Lowe

SEPTEMBER 2011
HARDBACK TITLES

ROMANCE

The Kanellis Scandal	Michelle Reid
Monarch of the Sands	Sharon Kendrick
One Night in the Orient	Robyn Donald
His Poor Little Rich Girl	Melanie Milburne
The Sultan's Choice	Abby Green
The Return of the Stranger	Kate Walker
Girl in the Bedouin Tent	Annie West
Once Touched, Never Forgotten	Natasha Tate
Nice Girls Finish Last	Natalie Anderson
The Italian Next Door...	Anna Cleary
From Daredevil to Devoted Daddy	Barbara McMahon
Little Cowgirl Needs a Mum	Patricia Thayer
To Wed a Rancher	Myrna Mackenzie
Once Upon a Time in Tarrula	Jennie Adams
The Secret Princess	Jessica Hart
Blind Date Rivals	Nina Harrington
Cort Mason – Dr Delectable	Carol Marinelli
Survival Guide to Dating Your Boss	Fiona McArthur

HISTORICAL

The Lady Gambles	Carole Mortimer
Lady Rosabella's Ruse	Ann Lethbridge
The Viscount's Scandalous Return	Anne Ashley
The Viking's Touch	Joanna Fulford

MEDICAL ROMANCE™

Return of the Maverick	Sue MacKay
It Started with a Pregnancy	Scarlet Wilson
Italian Doctor, No Strings Attached	Kate Hardy
Miracle Times Two	Josie Metcalfe

SEPTEMBER 2011
LARGE PRINT TITLES

ROMANCE

Too Proud to be Bought	Sharon Kendrick
A Dark Sicilian Secret	Jane Porter
Prince of Scandal	Annie West
The Beautiful Widow	Helen Brooks
Rancher's Twins: Mum Needed	Barbara Hannay
The Baby Project	Susan Meier
Second Chance Baby	Susan Meier
Her Moment in the Spotlight	Nina Harrington

HISTORICAL

More Than a Mistress	Ann Lethbridge
The Return of Lord Conistone	Lucy Ashford
Sir Ashley's Mettlesome Match	Mary Nichols
The Conqueror's Lady	Terri Brisbin

MEDICAL ROMANCE™

Summer Seaside Wedding	Abigail Gordon
Reunited: A Miracle Marriage	Judy Campbell
The Man with the Locked Away Heart	Melanie Milburne
Socialite...or Nurse in a Million?	Molly Evans
St Piran's: The Brooding Heart Surgeon	Alison Roberts
Playboy Doctor to Doting Dad	Sue MacKay

BV